Enrollment Form

☐ **Yes!** I WANT TO BE A *Privileged Woman*.

Enclosed is one *PAGES & PRIVILEGES*™ Proof of Purchase from any Harlequin or Silhouette book currently for sale in stores (Proofs of Purchase are found on the back pages of books) and the store cash register receipt. Please enroll me in *PAGES & PRIVILEGES*™. Send my Welcome Kit and FREE Gifts – and activate my FREE benefits – immediately.

More great gifts and benefits to come.

_____

NAME (please print)

_____

ADDRESS   APT. NO

_____

CITY   STATE   ZIP/POSTAL CODE

PROOF OF PURCHASE ONLY

NO CLUB!
NO COMMITMENT!
Just one purchase brings you great Free Gifts and Benefits!

Please allow 6-8 weeks for delivery. Quantities are limited. We reserve the right to substitute items. Enroll before October 31, 1995 and receive one full year of benefits.

Name of store where this book was purchased_____

Date of purchase_____

Type of store:
☐ Bookstore   ☐ Supermarket   ☐ Drugstore
☐ Dept. or discount store (e.g. K-Mart or Walmart)
☐ Other (specify)_____

Which Harlequin or Silhouette series do you usually read?

_____

Complete and mail with one Proof of Purchase and store receipt to:

U.S.: *PAGES & PRIVILEGES*™, P.O. Box 1960, Danbury, CT 06813-1960

Canada: *PAGES & PRIVILEGES*™, 49-6A The Donway West, P.O. 813, North York, ON M3C 2E8

SSE-PP6B

▶ DETACH HERE AND MAIL TODAY! ▶

"You know what I wish?"

Mitch said softly.

"What?"

"I wish Nicholas was our son. Yours and mine. I've always wished that. Sometimes at night, when I'd go in his room to kiss him good-night, I'd pretend he was. I'd pretend that when I left him and went into my bedroom, you'd be there." He made a funny, self-deprecating sound. "You probably think I'm nuts, but I would have given anything to have you be the mother of my son."

Eve could feel the tears forming in the backs of her eyes. *Oh, Mitch, I'm so sorry. So very sorry.*

"Hurry back, will you?" he murmured. "I've spent too much time without you already. I don't want to spend any more time apart."

Dear Reader,

There's a lot in store for you this month from Silhouette Special Edition! We begin, of course, with October's THAT SPECIAL WOMAN! title, *D Is for Dani's Baby*, by Lisa Jackson. It's another heartwarming and emotional installment in her LOVE LETTERS series. Don't miss it!

We haven't seen the last of Morgan Trayhern as Lindsay McKenna returns with a marvelous new series, MORGAN'S MERCENARIES: LOVE AND DANGER. You'll want to be there for every spine-tingling and passionately romantic tale, and it all starts with *Morgan's Wife*. And for those of you who have been eagerly following the delightful ALWAYS A BRIDESMAID! series, look no further, as Katie Jones is able to say she's *Finally a Bride*, by Sherryl Woods.

Also this month, it's city girl versus roguish rancher in *A Man and a Million*, by Jackie Merritt. A second chance at love—and a secret long kept—awaits in *This Child Is Mine*, by Trisha Alexander. And finally, October is Premiere month, and we're pleased to welcome new author Laurie Campbell and her story *And Father Makes Three*.

Next month we're beginning our celebration of Special Edition's 1000th book with some of your favorite authors! Don't miss books from Diana Palmer, Nora Roberts and Debbie Macomber—just to name a few! I know you'll enjoy the blockbuster months ahead. I hope you enjoy each and every story to come!

Sincerely,

Tara Gavin, Senior Editor

Please address questions and book requests to:
Silhouette Reader Service
U.S.: 3010 Walden Ave., P.O. Box 1325, Buffalo, NY 14269
Canadian: P.O. Box 609, Fort Erie, Ont. L2A 5X3

TRISHA ALEXANDER
THIS CHILD IS MINE

Silhouette®

SPECIAL EDITION®

Published by Silhouette Books
America's Publisher of Contemporary Romance

This book is dedicated to the memory of my parents, Pat and
Ann Sfara, who gave me the lasting gift of belief in myself,
and to my children—Kim Howard, Sandy Kay and
Shelley Kay—to whom the gift was passed on.

 SILHOUETTE BOOKS

ISBN 0-373-09989-4

THIS CHILD IS MINE

Books by Trisha Alexander

Silhouette Special Edition

Cinderella Girl #640
When Somebody Loves You #748
When Somebody Needs You #784
Mother of the Groom #801
When Somebody Wants You #822
Here Comes the Groom #845
Say You Love Me #875
What Will the Children Think? #906
Let's Make It Legal #924
The Real Elizabeth Hollister... #940
The Girl Next Door #965
This Child Is Mine #989

TRISHA ALEXANDER

has had a lifelong love affair with books and has always wanted to be a writer. She also loves cats, movies, the ocean, music, Broadway shows, cooking, traveling, being with her family and friends, Cajun food, Calvin and Hobbes and getting mail. Trisha and her husband have three grown children, two adorable grandchildren and live in Houston, Texas. Trisha loves to hear from readers. You can write to her at P.O. Box 441603, Houston, TX 77244-1603.

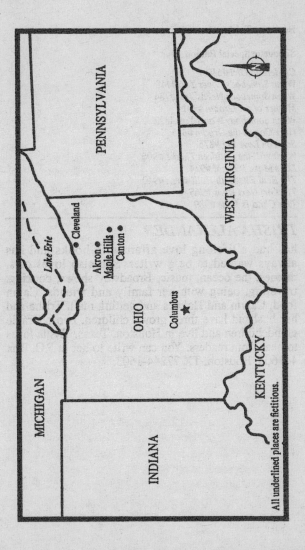

All underlined places are fictitious.

Chapter One

Eve DelVecchio sank back against the plush seat of the sleek gray limo and watched the driver expertly steer the vehicle through the maze of traffic coming and going from Port Columbus International Airport.

She stared out at the rolling Ohio landscape as the limo picked up speed and entered the ramp that would carry them to Interstate 71 heading north.

Heading toward Maple Hills.

Maple Hills, Ohio.

Population 17,322.

The town where Eve had been born and had lived for the first eighteen years of her life.

The town she had not visited in twenty years.

The town she had never expected to see again.

Had she made the right decision when she'd decided to come back? she wondered for at least the hundredth time since she'd sent her acceptance of the invitation to her twentieth high school reunion. Wouldn't it have been far wiser, far easier, to have remained in New York, where she had carved out a place for herself? A place that didn't include bitter and agonizing memories? A place that didn't include Mitchell Sinclair?

Eve sighed. Yes, perhaps it would have been smarter to leave well enough alone. Opening old wounds could be a painful process. And yet, if she were to build any kind of lasting relationship with a man, this trip was necessary. Because, no matter how she'd tried to put her past behind her, the last twenty years had not provided closure.

Mitchell Sinclair had continued to haunt her dreams. Although he had hurt her unbearably, in the years since they'd parted, she had continued to compare all other men to him. And all other men had come up short.

She knew she had probably built Mitch up to an impossible pinnacle. Because she'd been only seventeen when she'd fallen so wildly in love with him, she had made him out to be some kind of superman.

Yes, she thought. This trip was necessary. She needed to see that Mitch was just an ordinary human being. Probably fatter. Probably balding. Probably boring.

Only then would she be able to move on.

And although it was a secondary consideration, it would also give her the greatest pleasure to have the town fathers groveling at her feet. To see their wives falling all over each other for the privilege of entertaining her: Eve DelVecchio, the talented, beautiful and successful fashion designer whose upscale label Eden was worn by every up-and-coming professional woman in the country. The same Eve DelVecchio who had grown up on the wrong side of the Maple Hills tracks.

"Ma'am, we'll be in Maple Hills in about five minutes," the driver said, eyeing her in the rearview mirror.

"Yes, I know." Eve opened her handbag, removed an eighteen-karat gold compact studded with pavé diamonds and aquamarines, her signature jewel, and proceeded to powder her nose. She looked at herself critically in the mirror and smoothed down a few stray strands of hair that had escaped its careful pageboy styling.

Eve's dark hair, which was almost black, was thick and lustrous and showed no signs of gray. Her wide eyes, slightly tilted at the corners and a shade of blue gray that a former Scottish lover had once said reminded him of the heather on the moors in his homeland, were her best feature, and she knew it. Now, as she inspected herself, she decided she needed just a touch more eye shadow to emphasize their unusual color.

After applying the shadow and fresh lipstick, she took out the tiny atomizer of Temptation, the enormously successful fragrance she'd introduced the previous year, and spritzed herself. She adjusted the rolled collar of her slate blue, raw silk suit and straightened the crescent-shaped aquamarine-and-diamond brooch gracing her left lapel. She noted with satisfaction how the ten-karat aquamarine ring adorning her left hand sparkled in the sunlight slanting through the limo's windows.

Smiling, pleased with her appearance and knowing she'd cause the stir she wanted, she snapped her compact shut and slipped it back into her silk handbag.

Although she'd thought she was ready for it, when the sign proclaiming Maple Hills, A Friendly Place To

Live, suddenly loomed into view as the limo crested a hill, she couldn't prevent a tiny leap of her heart. She took a deep breath, irritated with herself. There was no reason to be nervous.

After all, in the past dozen years she had met senators and movie stars, famous hostesses and royalty. She was even on a first-name basis with a former president. Nothing Maple Hills had to offer could compare to that.

She told herself all of this as the driver exited the interstate and turned right. *Remember who you are. Remember what you've accomplished. Think of how envious they're all going to be—all those people who always thought they were too good for you and your family.*

"Do you know how to get to the Maple Hills Inn?" the driver asked, "or should I stop for directions?"

"I know how to get there." She should know how to get there. Her older brother Tony had once worked there as kitchen help. "Just keep going straight on this road until you get to Market Square. Once you're past the square, turn left at the first street which is Main, then right on Willow Road, then left on Maple Avenue. I'll show you."

Dozens of emotions tumbled through Eve's mind as the big car slowly traversed the town. She looked out the tinted back windows and noted how, on the surface at least, little had changed. The bandstand occupying the place of honor in the middle of the village green since the second year of the town's existence looked exactly the same—gleaming white and surrounded by beds of pansies in vivid yellows and purples.

Omar's Hardware Store and Dancy's Diner still stood side by side on Market Square. And The Malt Shop, the favorite hangout of the high school crowd, still had its window boxes filled with geraniums and its red-striped awning and wrought iron tables and chairs, in Maple Hills's imitation of a Paris sidewalk café.

Eve swallowed over the heavy lump in her throat as the driver turned off Market Square and onto Main Street. In the middle of the block where her father's tiny shoe repair shop used to be, there was now a real estate agency. She glanced up at the second story, saw that the sign in the window said Jason Weatherby, Insurance. She closed her eyes for a long moment, fighting the memories, fighting the pain.

She and her parents had lived upstairs, over the shop, from the time Eve was a little girl. Every day, after school, she would spend the hours until her father closed the shop perched on a wooden stool in the back room. Even now, just thinking about those days, she could smell the shoe polish and leather and that peculiar odor, not unpleasant, of all the feet that had walked in all the shoes.

She would raptly watch her father work and ask him incessant questions.

"Why are you taking that sole off, Papa?"

"What's that, Papa?"

"Who does that shoe belong to, Papa?"

"Will you buy me a pair of shoes like that, Papa?"

And Giovanni DelVecchio would patiently answer all of his adored daughter's questions.

"I have to take the sole off, my angel. How can I fix the shoe if I don't?"

"This shoe? It belongs to Mrs. Merriman."

"You're too little to wear shoes like this, my angel, but someday, when you're grown up, you will."

Sometimes the questions concerned schoolwork. "Ask your mama," her father would usually say. "You know I'm not very smart when it comes to your studies."

"You're the smartest papa in the world," Eve would loyally insist, and her father would smile, his beautiful dark eyes filled with love as they rested on her face.

Eve had always known how much Mama and Papa loved her. Mama had told her so, over and over again. "Your papa and I," Angela would say, "had given up hope of having more children. Then, when Tony was fifteen, like a miracle, through the grace of God, you came along."

Angela had been forty-five when Eve was born, and it had been a difficult birth. Giovanni, fifty-two, had been terrified he would lose his wife. But she pulled through and lived until Eve was twenty. Eve's father died three years after his wife.

Eve still missed them. They had been strict, old-fashioned parents, but they had lavished love and attention on her. They had been inordinately proud of her, too. Proud of her beauty and sparkling personality, but more proud of her intelligence and the good grades she got in school. Like many first-generation Americans, they valued education above all things and saw in Eve a chance to have a doctor or a lawyer in the family.

The fact that Eve was more interested in art and literature didn't faze them at all. "She can do everything," Angela would brag to her Altar Society friends. "Look at her. Isn't she wonderful?"

Yes, Eve thought, her parents *had* thought she was wonderful. They'd expected great things of her. They'd believed she could do no wrong. She grimaced. She had disappointed them terribly. Her deepest regret was that neither one had lived long enough to know that, in the end, she had overcome her disastrous beginning and had made something of herself. Something that she was sure would have made them proud again.

The limousine turned right onto Willow Road, so named because of the dozens of weeping willow trees in the esplanade. They passed Willow Road Elementary School about a half mile down on the right, and again the memories crowded in on Eve. She had spent seven happy years at Willow Road Elementary, and during those years her mother had worked in the school cafeteria.

As the big car slowly navigated the broad street, heading east, she prepared herself for the last hurdle before they reached the Maple Hills Inn.

She saw Porter Woods coming up on the left, and her heart started to pound. "This next street is Maple Avenue," she said. The driver nodded and turned left. The woods continued for several hundred yards, and then...yes, there it was, the open stretch of field where, the first weekend of June, St. Ignatius Church held its annual festival.

Eve wanted to look away, but she couldn't. All her lectures to herself faded from her mind, and she stared at the place where, twenty years ago, a meeting had taken place that had completely altered the direction of her life.

Friday, June third, twenty years earlier

"Eve, what time are you leaving for the festival?"

Eve tied the ends of her black halter top around her neck. "Jamie's coming by at six o'clock," she called out. She looked at herself critically in the mirror. Would her mother let her get away with wearing the halter top? Or would she insist Eve put on something that would expose less skin?

Eve twisted this way and that, admiring the way the halter top hugged her figure and made her breasts seem fuller.

Eve smiled. Yes, the halter top was perfect with her black-and-white skirt, one of those new long ones with a slit up the side. She'd had to fight with Mama over the purchase of the skirt, but she'd finally won, although Mama had continued to mutter under her breath.

"But at least it's *long,* Mama," Eve had said when Angela first objected to it. "You didn't like the mini-skirts, so I thought you'd like this one."

"You keep that opening buttoned up," Angela re-torted, her blue eyes worried. "Boys nowadays have only one thing on their minds."

"Oh, Mama," Eve said. Her mother was convinced if she and Eve's father neglected, for even one mo-ment, their strict supervision of Eve, disaster could strike. Although Eve loved her parents and understood their concern, she wanted to be like the other girls, and she wished she didn't have to fight so hard for every-thing she wanted.

Now, as Eve looked at herself, she knew her argu-ments in favor of the skirt had been worth it. She looked grown-up in it.

Grown-up and . . . sexy.

She stared at herself, taking a deep breath and let-ting it out slowly. Yes. She definitely looked sexy.

Her gaze, pulled by forces she was only beginning to acknowledge, settled on the swell of her breasts. She wondered what it would be like to do it. Jamie had done it. She'd had sex with Rick Munchack, and she'd told Eve about some of it, smiling that self-satisfied smile that made Eve feel completely left out.

"I liked it best when he touched me down there," Jamie had whispered. "That was far out."

Eve swallowed, remembering, shivering as she felt her nipples pucker from the images Jamie's recalled words conjured in her mind. She squeezed her legs together as something coiled deep inside.

Forcing the delicious thoughts from her mind, Eve hurriedly turned from the mirror. Her cheeks felt warm. She wondered what her mother would say if she'd known what Eve had been thinking. She'd probably ground Eve for the rest of her life.

A few minutes later—composed again—Eve left her small bedroom and walked down the hall to the kitchen. Their apartment above her father's shop wasn't very big. Just a living room, kitchen, bathroom and two bedrooms—one large and one small.

Eve constantly fought her feelings of guilt because her home wasn't a place where she felt comfortable inviting her school friends. Jamie came all the time, of course, but Jamie's father worked in the ceramics factory on the outskirts of town, and her family didn't have any more money or education than Eve's.

The rest of Eve's school friends were different. Their fathers were professionals who either worked here in Maple Hills or commuted to Columbus. Doctors, lawyers, accountants, computer experts, a couple of professors who taught at Ohio State University.

Eve's father was a shoemaker. Eve wasn't ashamed of her father—no, of course, she wasn't—but she couldn't make herself invite the Nicholls twins, for instance, to her apartment. She could just imagine how Sarah Nicholls's small nose would quiver at the ever-present smell of garlic permeating the rooms and how Shawn Nicholls's eyes would shine with amusement at the lurid painting of Jesus with his bleeding heart that hung in prominent display on the DelVecchio living room wall.

Even the thought made Eve shudder. Most of her school friends—although they probably would never say or do anything in Eve's presence to let her know how they felt—would quietly snicker over the way Eve lived. Worse, they'd discuss her behind her back. At their country club dances and during their tennis lessons they would laugh about her parents and her home.

Eve would die if that happened. She couldn't help it. She loved her parents, but they were so much older than her friends' parents and they had clung to the old-country ways. Although they had come to the United States as children, somehow they had never adapted to the more modern ways of thinking and living. As far as they were concerned, things like the sexual revolution might have happened on another planet, because it certainly had not altered their thinking or touched their lives in any way.

Eve sighed. More than anything in the world, she wanted to be one of the in crowd at Maple Hills High School. Eve knew the only reason those girls even acknowledged her existence was because she was smart. She had been elected to the National Honor Society as well as the student council.

But she wasn't *really* a part of the crowd and she never would be. She wished she didn't care, but secretly, in her heart of hearts, she wanted to be exactly like them. She wanted to belong to the Methodist church and go to Sunday school and be a Rainbow Girl.

She wanted to live in a two-story, redbrick house with a circular driveway and an acre of lawn surrounding it. She wanted a mother who wore suits and pearls and played bridge and golf. She wanted a father who didn't speak with an accent and who didn't mend other people's shoes. She wanted to go away to college and be rushed by the best sorority and go skiing in Vermont over the Thanksgiving holidays.

None of those things was ever going to happen. Eve knew that, and for the most part, she had accepted it. Still, there were times, like now, when she couldn't help wishing her parents would at least join the decade of the seventies.

As Eve entered the kitchen, her mother, who was standing at the stove frying pork chops with green peppers, turned. Immediately a frown creased Angela's round face, which was shiny with perspiration.

Eve pretended not to see the frown. She reached into the bowl of salad that stood on the countertop next to the sink and picked out a large black olive. "Mmm. I hope Jamie hurries. I'm starving."

Eve had hoped to distract her mother, but it didn't work, for Angela said, "I don't like that halter you've got on. Go and change it for something decent."

"Mama . . ."

"I mean it, Eve."

Eve sighed.

"And put on a bra."

"You can't wear a bra with a halter top, Mama."

"Yes. My point exactly." Angela deftly turned the thick chops with a two-tined fork.

"But Mama, it's so hot today."

"So wear a cool cotton blouse." Angela reached for the pepper and liberally sprinkled the food in the frying pan.

"My white blouse is dirty."

"So wear your black sleeveless blouse."

"It's dirty, too," Eve lied, crossing her fingers behind her back.

"Eve . . . if you're lying to me . . ."

"I'm not, Mama. I'm not. I'll show you."

Eve raced back to her bedroom and grabbed the black blouse from its hanger. Kneeling down, she reached for her tennis shoes, which were caked with mud. Smiling guiltily, she rubbed the sole of one of the shoes against the front of the blouse. After two or three swipes, she crumpled the blouse up to wrinkle it, then marched back to the kitchen and triumphantly held the blouse aloft for her mother to see.

Angela's eyes, so like Eve's, studied her thoughtfully. Finally her gaze dropped to the long black scarf Eve had tied around her waist. "Put that scarf around your shoulders."

Eve grinned. "Okay, Mama."

Just then Eve heard the door at the bottom of the stairs open and shut, then the clatter of Jamie's feet as she raced upstairs. "Eve? You ready?"

"Ready."

Eve kissed her mother. "Bye, Mama. I'll be home by midnight." Midnight was Eve's curfew, and she knew better than to stretch it.

Angela gripped Eve's arm. "Eve, remember what I've always told you?"

"I know, I know."

"I mean it. If a boy tries to touch you, you push his hands away. Boys, that's all they think about."

Eve rolled her eyes, and she and Jamie exchanged a grin. Eve's parents lectured her at every opportunity about chastity and purity and wearing a white dress when she was married. If Eve had heard it once, she'd heard it a thousand times. Nice girls didn't. Good girls didn't.

And so far, their warnings had paid off, for Eve hadn't seriously considered having sex with a boy. Nor had any boy touched her.

Well, Bill O'Toole had fondled her breast last year when she'd allowed him to kiss her behind the bleachers, but she'd quickly shoved his hand away, even as her breast tingled from the contact.

Eve could feel her cheeks warming as she remembered how she'd touched herself that night, secretly, under the covers. She hurriedly thrust the memory aside. She wasn't proud of herself for yielding to her curiosity and the almost compelling need to find out what the other girls were talking about when they giggled and whispered.

"Don't worry, Mama," she said, extricating herself from her mother's grip. "I know how to take care of myself."

Chapter Two

Mitchell Sinclair stared at the telephone.

So she was really here.

Right here in Maple Hills.

After all these years, he was finally going to see Eve DelVecchio again. He hadn't quite believed it when he'd heard she was coming back for her class reunion. Even after he'd received the invitation to the reception that Terry Flynn, the newly elected mayor of Maple Hills, was hosting, Mitch hadn't allowed himself to dwell on the possibility of her return, because he was sure something would happen to prevent her from coming.

Slowly he replaced the receiver.

Eve.

From the first moment he'd set eyes on her, he'd been captivated. She was the most enchanting girl he'd ever met, and he'd never forgotten her. Even now, twenty years later, all he had to do was close his eyes and there she was, just as vivid as if she were standing in front of him.

Her eyes—not blue, not gray, but an unforgettable combination. Her smile—sparkling with joy and totally irresistible. Her hair—like clouds of dark silk floating around her exquisite face.

God, she'd been beautiful.

When he was with her, he'd forgotten everything and everyone but her. She'd made him feel ten feet tall, as if he could move mountains. She'd made him happier than he'd ever been, before or since.

Mitch stood restlessly. He walked to his office window which overlooked Main Street, and gazed down.

He would see her tomorrow night.

He wondered how she would act, what she would say. Would she even remember him?

The thought that she might not, that what had happened between them so many years ago had not been important enough to remember, hurt more than he wanted to admit.

Why should she want to remember you? All you ever did was hurt her. Hurt her and abandon her after promising to love her forever.

Regret and guilt crept through him as the question that had haunted him for twenty years came back to haunt him again.

What else could he have done?

Friday, June third, twenty years earlier

Mitch tucked his green shirt into the waistband of his jeans and zipped them up.

"So what do you want to do tonight?" he asked his best friend, Kevin McBride, who was leaning against the door frame of Mitch's bedroom.

"I kinda thought we could check out that festival."

Mitch frowned. "What festival?" He shoved his feet into his sneakers and bent down to tie them.

"You know. The one over at Maple Field. It's put on by some church."

"Oh, yeah..." Mitch straightened up. "What's the big deal about that?" He had never attended one of those festivals, even when he was in high school, and now he was a first-year law student, soon to be second year. "Won't it just be a bunch of kids?"

Kevin grinned. "Some of those high school girls are really stacked...." He used his hands to illustrate his point, his grin turning into a leer.

Mitch rolled his eyes. "Jeez, McBride, you've really got a one-track mind."

"Hey, I'm not gettin' any on a regular basis like you are...."

Kevin's taunt made Mitch feel uneasy. He wished he'd never revealed any details about his relationship with Carolyn Whittaker. He had regretted the confidence immediately after sharing it, but once he had, he couldn't take the words back.

"It's not like that," he said.

"Well, sure, that's because she's in Europe now. But when she comes home, it'll be a different story. She'll be all over you, and you know it."

Mitch had no answer for this, because he knew Kevin's statement was true. In fact, Carolyn had initiated the sexual intimacy between them. And even though, by then, Mitch had started having doubts about their relationship, he hadn't been able to refuse what she was offering. There was too much guilt on his part. He felt sorry for her, and in some way, he'd felt an obligation to make things up to her, even though nothing that had happened had been Mitch's fault.

His family and Carolyn's family went back a long way. Their fathers were very close friends, as well as business associates. His mother and Carolyn's mother had grown up together. His mother had been Carolyn's mother's maid of honor, and Carolyn's mother was Mitch's godmother.

And Carolyn had once been Cliff's girl.

Mitch could never think about Cliff without feeling an emptiness and overwhelming sense of loss. From the time Mitch was a little kid, he had adored his big brother. Even though Cliff was only three years older than Mitch, he had seemed larger than life. Mitch had followed Cliff around like a puppy dog. He had wanted to be just like Cliff—who was smart and brave and a natural-born leader.

Everything Cliff did, Mitch wanted to do, too.

When Cliff got his first two-wheeler, Mitch was determined to learn how to ride one so he could go where Cliff went.

When Cliff got his driver's license, Mitch couldn't wait until he turned sixteen so he could get his, too.

Cliff had been casually indulgent and had usually let Mitch tag along after him.

It was only when Cliff started to show an interest in girls that Mitch was naturally left behind.

He sighed heavily. All that was changed now, of course. Everything was changed ever since that one awful night when Cliff had wrapped his new sports car around a tree and died at Maple Hills General Hospital three days later.

"Hey, Mitch . . ." Kevin said, breaking into Mitch's thoughts. "Something wrong?"

Mitch shook off the memories. "No, I'm okay." He grabbed his wallet from the dresser and shoved it into his back pocket. He eyed his keys. "You driving?"

"Why don't we both drive?" Kevin suggested.

"Why take two cars?"

"Well," Kevin drawled, "maybe I'll get lucky."

Mitch laughed. "Yeah, knowing you, you probably will. Okay. I'll drive, too. Where did you say this festival was?"

"Out at Maple Field, you know, just past Porter Woods."

"Oh. Yeah."

The two boys walked down the hall to the den. Mitch's mother was watching "The Mary Tyler Moore Show," and looked up as they entered the room.

"Bye, Mrs. Sinclair," Kevin said.

"Goodbye, Kevin."

Mitch leaned over and kissed her cheek. "Bye, Mom."

"Don't be too late," she said, "and be careful driving."

"I will," Mitch said automatically.

Outside, he said goodbye to his father, who was standing in the driveway talking to their next-door neighbor. Then he climbed into his red Mustang convertible and took off.

As he drove toward the festival site, Mitch's thoughts slid gloomily back to Carolyn and his relationship with her. For some time now, he'd entertained the traitorous idea of breaking off with her. He knew the idea was traitorous, because he had allowed Carolyn to think he wanted to marry her. They weren't officially engaged, or anything, but when she'd talked about the future, he had never contradicted her.

Official engagement or not, their families expected the two of them to marry, too.

How had things gone this far?

In the beginning, he and Carolyn had naturally gravitated toward each other. They were both hurting. They had both loved Cliff, and they comforted each other. When and how their relationship had changed, Mitch had no idea. It all just seemed to happen.

One night about six months after Cliff's death, they'd been sitting on the couch in Carolyn's living room. They'd been talking about Cliff, and she had started to cry. Mitch put his arm around her, and the next thing he knew, she had nuzzled her face against his neck, and before he had time to think, he was kissing her.

After that, things snowballed. And Mitch did nothing to stop them. He'd often wondered why. Down deep, in the darkest part of himself, had he felt that by taking Cliff's girl, he'd be taking Cliff's place? Had he wanted to be Cliff?

Mitch guessed he'd never know what forces had driven him. One thing he did know, though. He didn't love Carolyn the way a man should love the woman he planned to marry.

And it was past time to do something about it.

"Oh, Miss DelVecchio, we're so *honored* to have you staying with us," the manager of the Maple Hills Inn gushed. "We've already received just *dozens* of messages for you!" Giving her an ingratiating smile, the manager handed her several pink message slips and two white envelopes. A short man whose name tag identified him as Walter French, he puffed up as tall as he possibly could and gestured to the bellboy, a wide-eyed redhead with a punk haircut. "Todd, show Miss DelVecchio to the Presidential Suite. Hurry up, now!"

Eve smothered a smile. The Presidential Suite, indeed. And just when did the obsequious Mr. French expect a president to visit a town as inconsequential as Maple Hills? Well, actually, she guessed she qualified. After all, she was president and CEO of DelVecchio Designs.

As the bellboy loaded her bags onto a luggage cart, Eve finished checking in, then followed the bellboy to the elevator. It was only when she heard, "Be careful now, watch your step," from behind her that she realized Mr. French was still with them.

He talked nonstop all the way to the top floor, the sixth, and continued his nervous chatter until they reached Eve's suite, located at the very end of the long hallway.

"Allow me," he said, producing an ornate key—no coded plastic here—and unlocked the double walnut doors, throwing them wide.

Eve looked around with satisfaction. The suite was really lovely, as nice as any she'd inhabited since making her mark in the world of fashion. Decorated in soft shades of peach and gray and filled with delicate antiques, the rooms were inviting and restful.

An enormous bouquet of deep red roses sat on top of a small rosewood writing desk. Next to the flowers was a Waterford candy dish filled with Godiva chocolates. A round serving table held a cellophane-covered tray of cheeses, crackers and fruit, and next to it a wine bucket contained a chilling bottle of champagne.

Mr. French's gaze darted around the room, obviously checking every detail. "I do hope everything is to your liking, Miss DelVecchio."

"Everything is very nice. Thank you."

The bellboy removed her luggage from the cart, laying the largest of her suitcases across the webbed luggage holder. Eve tipped him generously, and he grinned. "Gee, thanks."

"If there's anything else you need . . ." Mr. French showed no signs of leaving.

"No, thank you. I'm sure everything is fine. All I really want now is to unpack," Eve said firmly. Surely he'd take the hint. She slipped her jacket off.

"Of course, of course. But you'll call me if there's anything you want, won't you? Now, come on, Todd. Let's leave Miss DelVecchio alone." Still sputtering and fussing like an oversolicitous mother, Mr. French handed Eve the key to the suite, then guided the bellboy out of the room.

Sighing in relief, Eve sank down on the peach-and-cream-striped satin sofa and rifled through the messages. The first was from the mayor, who was having a reception in her honor the following evening and wanted to talk to her about it.

Then there were two with vaguely familiar women's names, probably women she'd gone to school with.

The next bore the name Mrs. Beardsley. Eve grinned in delight. Lorraine Beardsley had been her art teacher in high school, and Eve had loved her. It would be wonderful to see her again.

The last was from Jamie. Jamie Zimmerman. Eve's best friend throughout high school. Jamie, whom Eve hadn't seen since that fateful night at the St. Ignatius Festival.

Eve set the messages aside. She'd call everyone a little later. She slit open the first of the two envelopes. It
was another message from Mayor Flynn.

Dear Miss DelVecchio
I am looking forward to seeing you tomorrow evening and would be happy to send a driver to pick
you up. Just let my secretary know.

>   With all best wishes,
>   Terence Flynn

She chuckled. Mayor Flynn would probably send
something ostentatious, like a white limo. Well, why
not? It would be fun to cause a stir.

She looked curiously at the second envelope, addressed in flowery, feminine handwriting. She quickly
slit the envelope open and looked at the message. Eve's
heart shot up into her throat as the signature jumped
out at her.

Pamela Sinclair. Mitch Sinclair's mother.

Eve quickly scanned the neatly penned message.

You're invited to attend a luncheon at my home on
Sunday afternoon. It'll just be a small group of
women who want to welcome you to our town. We
do hope you can join us.

>   Pamela Sinclair
>   (Mrs. Clifford Sinclair)

There was a telephone number under her name.

Eve stared.

Mitch Sinclair's mother wouldn't have given Eve the
time of day twenty years ago. In fact, if Pamela had
known about her son's involvement with Eve, she would

probably have moved heaven and earth to put an end to it. And she certainly would never have considered inviting the shoemaker's daughter into her home.

Eve wondered what Pamela Sinclair would do now if she knew the truth. Would she still want Eve to be her guest of honor on Sunday? Somehow Eve doubted it.

Eve stood and walked slowly over to the wall of windows and gazed out. This side of the hotel overlooked Maple Field and Porter Woods, and beyond the woods, just off to her right, Porter Lake.

A funny, achy feeling hollowed her stomach as she stared at the distant patch of blue.

All those nights she and Mitch had spent parked by the lake, most of them wonderful, one of them terrible, tumbled in her mind in a kaleidoscope of images.

Even now, so many years later, she could still smell the popcorn and greasy hamburgers and fries, still taste the sticky sweetness of cotton candy and candied apples, still feel the moist heat of the June night, still see the bobbing lanterns and swirl of color as the merry-go-round circled in its ceaseless journey, still hear the organ music mixed with the shouts of vendors hawking their wares and the noise generated by hundreds of festival-goers.

She stared out the window for a long time.

Friday, June third, twenty years earlier

"Jamie, who's that boy over there?"

"Which one?" Jamie accepted the hot dog she'd just purchased from a vendor and took a bite. Mustard oozed from the end and she hurriedly licked it.

"I don't want to point," Eve said, inclining her head in the direction of the game booths. "He's got on a green shirt and jeans and he's shooting targets at the last booth.''

Jamie took another large bite, her dark eyes searching through the crowd. She grinned. "Oh, yeah. I see 'im. That's Mitch Sinclair. You know, the mayor's son. Cute, isn't he?''

Eve nodded. He was extremely cute. Tall and tanned, with medium blond hair and a nice build, shown to advantage in his tight jeans. "How old is he? I don't remember ever seeing him around.''

"I don't know. About twenty-two, maybe twenty-three," Jamie said around another huge mouthful of hot dog. "He's in law school, I think, 'cause Lindsay McBride mentioned him one day. I think that's her brother Kevin standing next to him." Jamie grinned. "He's cute, too.''

Eve gave Kevin McBride a cursory glance. She didn't care for his type—dark with slicked-back hair and a cocky stance. "He's okay." Her gaze returned to Mitch Sinclair, who had obviously just hit his target, if his whoop and delighted grin were any indication.

Even from this distance, Eve could see that he had a great smile, with big dimples cutting long grooves in his cheeks. He reminded her of her very favorite actor, Robert Redford.

"C'mon. Let's walk over there and talk to them," Jamie said, finishing off her hot dog and wiping her mouth on a napkin that she absently tossed in the direction of a trash container, missing it by inches.

Eve hurriedly shook her head. "Nuh-uh, they're too old for us." She could just imagine what her parents would say if she started hanging out with a boy five or six years older than she.

As it was, her parents had wanted her to wait until she was eighteen to even think about dating. It had taken a lot of talking and some intervention by Eve's older brother Anthony to bargain them down to seventeen.

"Speak for yourself," Jamie said. "I'm eighteen, which makes me old enough to drink, vote, and go out with anyone I darn well please!" She poked Eve with her elbow, grinning slyly. "When're you gonna cut the cord, huh, DelVecchio?"

Jamie never missed a chance to rub it in that she was almost a whole year older than Eve, who wouldn't turn eighteen until October.

She also never missed a chance to get in her digs about Eve's old-fashioned parents and the way Eve allowed them to rule her life.

Eve couldn't help it. Although she chafed at the restrictions her parents placed on her, she wanted to please them. She never wanted to disappoint them.

Jamie grabbed her hand. "C'mon," she said, charging off and dragging Eve along. "Live dangerously for once in your life."

Both boys turned as Jamie sidled up to them. "Hey! Great shot!" The remark was addressed to Mitch Sinclair, but it was Kevin McBride who received the benefit of Jamie's flirty smile. His dark eyes gave her an appreciative once-over.

"Thanks," Mitch Sinclair said. He smiled at Jamie, then trained his friendly hazel eyes on Eve. "Hi," he said softly.

Eve knew her cheeks were stained pink. She looked up into Mitch Sinclair's eyes, wishing she could think of something clever to say. "Hi."

"I'm Kevin, this is Mitch," said Kevin McBride. "And who are you two gorgeous creatures?"

"I'm Jamie," Jamie said in her sultriest Carly Simon voice. "This is my friend, Eve."

"Well, Jamie, would you like to ride the Ferris wheel with me?" Kevin said.

"You bet," Jamie said, laughing as Kevin draped his arm across her shoulders and led her off.

Mitch seemed kind of embarrassed, which made Eve feel better. She hoped he didn't think she was fast because she and Jamie had walked up to him and his friend like that. "Listen," she said hurriedly, "it was nice meeting you." She turned to go, stopping only as he caught her arm.

"Don't leave," he said. "We could go on the Ferris wheel, too. Or we could just walk around and talk."

His smile made her feel weak in the knees. He seemed awfully nice and a real gentleman, too. His eyes didn't rake her the way Kevin's eyes had raked Jamie.

"Okay," Eve said, forgetting that her parents wouldn't approve, forgetting everything except that Mitch was the cutest boy she'd ever seen and he was making her heart skip as he looked at her with frank admiration.

He laid down the target gun. "Which one? The Ferris wheel?"

Eve nodded. "Sure. That sounds like fun."

Just as they turned to leave, the man tending the booth said, "Hey, kid, don't ya want your prize?"

Mitch grinned sheepishly. "I forgot about it." He looked at her. "You pick one."

"Me?" Eve squeaked. What was wrong with her? she thought disgustedly. She was acting as if she'd never even talked to a boy before. Mitch probably thought she was a real dunce.

"Yeah. Pick the one you like."

Every time Mitch looked at her, Eve felt all fluttery inside. She was beginning to regret all the junk she'd eaten since she and Jamie arrived at the festival. She turned and looked at the row of prizes. There were dolls and stuffed animals. At the very end of the row was a huge white bunny. "That one," she said. "The bunny."

The man in the booth got the bunny down and handed it to her. "Oh, no, it's his," she said.

Mitch laughed. "What would I do with a stuffed animal? I want you to have it."

Eve smiled shyly. He *was* nice. She accepted the bunny. It felt soft in her arms, and she knew it was going to occupy a place of honor in her room.

They set off for the Ferris wheel, Mitch's hand lightly touching her waist. Suddenly everything about the night seemed unreal, and Eve wondered if she was dreaming. But no, Mitch was real. His hand at her waist was real. The warmth she felt through the thin fabric of her halter top was real. And the fluttery, excited feeling in her stomach was real, too.

The ride was magical: the velvety canopy of sky sprinkled with stars, the soft rush of the wind lifting their hair, the feeling that the two of them were the only people in the world, especially when their car stopped at the top, swaying back and forth gently.

"What's your last name?" Mitch said.

"DelVecchio."

"Do you go to Maple Hills High?"

"I used to. I graduated last month."

"Really? You don't look old enough to have graduated."

Oh, great. He thought she was a baby. "I'm almost eighteen." That wasn't really a lie. She would be eighteen in three and a half months. That was almost eighteen. "Where do you go to school?"

"I'm in law school at Yale."

"Jamie said she thought you were a law student." Eve could have kicked herself as soon as the words were out. Now he'd know they'd been talking about him. "H-how many years do you have left?"

Their car inched down one space as more people were loaded on the bottom. As it did, he casually draped his arm around the back of the car, not quite touching her bare back. Eve's breath caught as their gazes connected. She couldn't believe she was really sitting here with him.

"Two. How about you? Are you going to college?"

"Uh-huh. I'm planning to go to O.S.U." She didn't add that she would be living at home.

Just then the wheel began to move, and Mitch's arm tightened around her shoulders.

She looked up.

He looked down.

Eve's pulse went crazy as his gaze dropped to her mouth. For one breathless moment, she thought he was going to kiss her.

Time seemed to stand still. Slowly he raised his eyes, and their gazes met again. And Eve knew that even though he hadn't kissed her now—before the night was over, he would.

And she also knew she would let him.

Chapter Three

"Mr. Sinclair, you've got a call on line one. It's your mother."

"Thanks, Jill."

Mitch didn't immediately pick up the phone. He felt disoriented by the rush of memories he'd unleashed, and it took him a few seconds to pull himself out of the past and back to the present. As he reached for the receiver, he wondered what his mother wanted. She rarely disturbed him at work, so it must be important.

"Mitchell?" His mother's voice, always soft and carefully modulated, held an edge of excitement.

"Hi, Mom. What's up?"

"Oh, the most *delicious* thing," she gushed. "Joanna is going to be so *jealous!*"

Mitch grinned, wondering what social coup his mother had pulled off now. She and Joanna Whittaker, his former mother-in-law, were archrivals in spite of being lifelong friends. Dutifully playing his part, he said, "And why is she going to be jealous?"

"Because *I'm* hosting a luncheon on Sunday in honor of Eve DelVecchio, the designer who grew up in Maple Hills! And Joanna will be absolutely *green* when she finds out."

Mitch's mind reeled.

"She's always boasting about her friendship with Sybil London and acting as if I'm positively provincial because I'm not on a first-name basis with anybody famous. Well, I guess I'll show *her!*" Hardly pausing for breath, she gushed on. "I just got a call from Miss DelVecchio, and she was so lovely. She said she'd be delighted to come and was looking forward to it. And she even mentioned that she had fond memories of Maple Hills when your father was mayor. Isn't that wonderful? Oh, I can't *wait* until Joanna gets home from Europe. She'll be kicking herself because she wasn't here."

Mitch had finally gathered his wits enough to say, "That's great, Mom."

"Yes, isn't it? I don't suppose you know her, do you?"

"Who? Eve DelVecchio?"

"Yes. Oh, I know she's several years younger than you since the reason she's even here in Maple Hills is to attend her twentieth class reunion, but still...I thought you might have at least met her."

"Yes," Mitch said reluctantly, "I've met her."

"You *have?* Well, tell me what she's like. Do you think I should have Stella fix her wonderful shrimp casserole or do you think I should serve salmon?"

"Mom, we were kids when I met her. I have no idea what she's like now. Or what she likes to eat."

His mother laughed softly. "Oh, I know I'm being silly, but I do so want everything to be perfect."

"I'm sure it will be," Mitch said automatically.

"Have you been invited to the reception Terry Flynn's hosting tomorrow evening?"

Mitch's heart sank. Were his parents going to be there, too? It would be tough enough to see Eve again, but to have his parents there—possibly witnessing their reunion—would be hell. "Yes. Have you?"

"Yes, but your father and I are playing in that bridge tournament tomorrow and Saturday, and they're having a party for the participants tomorrow night, so we can't go."

"That's too bad."

"Yes, it *is* a shame, but I've got Sunday to look forward to."

"Yes."

"Tell me, have you heard from Nicholas lately?"

Mitch's fifteen-year-old son was spending a month in Europe with his Whittaker grandparents. "Yes," Mitch said, smiling as he always did at the mention of Nicholas, "I talked to him Sunday night."

"Where are they now?"

"They were in Rome on Sunday. But they were leaving for London Tuesday morning."

"Is Nicholas having a good time? Oh, I do so miss that boy!"

Mitch's parents were very close to Nicholas, as were Carolyn's parents. Nicholas was the only grandchild on both sides of the family, and the fact that he was a terrific kid certainly didn't hurt. "Yes, he's having a great time," Mitch said. "I could hardly shut him up, he was so excited."

"That's good...."

"Yes, I'm glad he's having fun." Mitch knew his mother was torn between wanting her beloved grandson to have a wonderful time on this trip and her ongoing rivalry with Joanna, intensified when it came to anything concerning Nicholas.

"I guess I should let you go. I know you're busy."

"Yes, I'm trying to get the Medlock contracts finished up today."

"Okay, well, have fun tomorrow night. And be sure and tell Miss DelVecchio how pleased I am that she's coming to the house on Sunday, won't you?"

"If I talk to her, I will."

"Of course, you'll talk to her. After all, you're going to the reception. Why *wouldn't* you talk to her?"

Mitch wished he'd just agreed with his mother. Why hadn't he? "I just meant that there'll be so many people there...you know..."

"Well, you make *sure* you talk to her. You just go up and introduce yourself. After all, your father used to be the mayor of Maple Hills, and *I'm* giving a luncheon in her honor on Sunday. I'm sure she would *expect* you to seek her out."

"Okay, Mom. I'll tell her what you said. Now I really have to go."

Long after they'd hung up, Mitch still hadn't shaken off the conversation, and despite the fact that he had told his mother the truth—he really did have a lot more work to get done that afternoon—he couldn't seem to stop thinking about tomorrow night and seeing Eve again.

A half hour later, he muttered, "Oh, hell," and shoved his paperwork aside. Swiveling his chair around to face the window, he propped his feet on the windowsill. He sat there a long time, staring out at the bright summer day, and let the memories come unhindered.

Friday, June third, twenty years earlier

Mitch knew he should tell Eve goodbye when the Ferris wheel ride was over. It was dangerous to spend any more time with her, because he liked her too much.

And he wasn't free to like a girl.

Until he broke off with Carolyn, he was as committed as if he really were engaged to her.

Regret filled him.

As soon as the ride ended, he'd better thank Eve, tell her it was nice meeting her, and then go home and out of temptation's path.

But when they stepped down from the car, she smiled up at him, and something happened to him, something that drove everything out of his mind except her and the way she made him feel. She had the most incredible smile, he thought, dazed by its effect on him.

And those eyes!

They were all shimmery and soft like the sky on a hazy summer's day. All his good resolutions forgotten, he heard himself say, "Would you like some ice cream or a hot dog or something?"

"Thanks, but I'm not hungry. Jamie and I've been eating ever since we got here."

"Well, how about a drink, then?" He was afraid she'd leave if he didn't think of a reason to keep her by his side, and suddenly it seemed like the most important thing in the world to keep her with him.

"All right." She smiled at him again. "I am a little thirsty."

His heart did a flip-flop. Jeez, what was wrong with him? He hadn't felt this way since he was thirteen and had such a painful crush on Jessica Button, the head junior high cheerleader and the most popular girl in his glass.

Mitch knew he wasn't being smart. What if someone who knew him and Carolyn should see him with Eve? What if Carolyn should find out about tonight before he had a chance to talk to her?

Okay. No real harm done yet. We'll just drink our drinks, then I really will say goodbye to her.

As he was lecturing himself, they walked to a nearby concession stand, and he bought them each a Coke. Then, sipping their drinks, they ambled over to one of the picnic tables set up at the fringes of the festival.

"This one okay?" he said, choosing the one farthest from the lights and people.

"Sure."

In unspoken agreement, they climbed up and sat on the table, feet resting on the bench. They sat a few feet apart, facing the crowd.

"So when do you go back to school?" she asked, giving him a sidelong look through her lashes. She sipped at her Coke.

Her voice was soft and husky—sexy, he thought—and she didn't giggle like so many of the girls her age seemed to do. Not that he'd had that much experience with younger girls. In fact, the only two he'd spent much time around were his cousin Heather, who would be a senior in high school this fall, and Kevin's sister Lindsay. But those two seemed to do nothing else but giggle—at least when he was around.

"The term doesn't start until the day after Labor Day," he said, "but I'll probably head on back to New

Haven a week or so before then. Get settled in the apartment and everything."

She nodded. "Do you have a roommate?"

"No. I did my first year, but it didn't work out well. Every time I wanted to study, he wanted to party. Anyway, my folks agreed with me that I was better off on my own."

She nodded again.

"What about you? When do you start school?"

"Orientation for the freshmen takes place the week before Labor Day, but we'll officially start the same day you do."

"Are you looking forward to it?"

"I can't wait." Her eyes shone.

He smiled at her eagerness, wishing he felt that excited about school. "What're you planning on studying?"

"Art. I—I want to be a fashion designer." The information was offered shyly.

"You must be talented. I've always wished I had some kind of talent." He liked the way she looked him directly in the eyes when she talked to him. She didn't flirt or act silly, either. He liked that, too. In fact, he liked everything about her.

She shrugged away his comment, but there was a pleased expression on her face. "But you're in law school. And at one of the best schools in the country. You must be really smart."

Now it was his turn to shrug. He'd always gotten good grades, that was true, but he never thought of himself as really smart. He just liked to read, he had a logical mind, and he had a very good memory.

"My dad always wanted to go to Yale. That's why I'm going there. I would have rather gone to O.S.U.," he confided, surprising himself. He'd never admitted that to anyone before.

She nodded thoughtfully. "Yeah, I know the feeling. I'd give anything to be able to go somewhere like the Parsons School of Design in New York or the Rhode Island School of Design."

He studied her face with its wistful expression. "Why don't you, then?"

She met his gaze squarely. "My family can't afford to send me somewhere like that, and even if they could, they wouldn't."

"Why not?"

She hesitated for a moment, as if considering whether or not she wanted to tell him. Then she gave a little shrug and said, "My parents are very old-fashioned. They think a girl shouldn't leave home until she gets married."

"Does that bother you?"

"Sometimes." She looked at him. "Does it bother you that you're going to a school your father chose instead of the one you'd rather go to?"

He smiled. "Sometimes." They were silent for a moment. "Have you ever told your folks how you feel?"

She shook her head. "No."

"Why not?"

She sighed. "It wouldn't do any good. They wouldn't change their minds, and then they'd be upset." Her gaze met his again. "I'd rather save my protests for something I have a prayer of winning."

Yeah, he knew what she meant. Some battles just weren't worth fighting. He studied her face, pensive now. In some ways, it was hard to believe she wasn't even eighteen yet. She seemed so mature, with a good head on her shoulders.

"How about you?" she asked. "Have you ever told your father how you feel?"

"No."

"Why not?"

He stared off into space. "It just wasn't that important. See, I... my folks, well, they've had so much disappointment and unhappiness." He swallowed. Even now, more than four years after Cliff's death, it was hard to talk about it. "My...my older brother died four years ago, just as he was about to start at Yale Law School."

"Oh, how terrible. What...what happened?"

"He wrapped his new sports car around a tree." Mitch would never forget that night. It was burned into his memory. The phone call at one in the morning. His mother's scream. His father's white face.

"Oh, God," she breathed.

Slowly he turned to look at her. Her eyes were filled with sympathy. She reached over and touched his forearm.

"I—I'm so sorry, Mitch," she said softly.

The warmth of her hand was comforting, and he could see she really understood how he felt. "Thanks."

"You miss him a lot, don't you?"

He nodded. "Do you ever question things? You know, like, if there's really a God, why does He allow things like this to happen?"

"Yes. I think everybody does."

"There aren't any answers, though."

They sat there silently for long moments. After a while, she said, "Do you have any other brothers or sisters?" She slowly removed her hand.

"No. There were just the two of us." He could still feel the imprint where her hand had been. "That's why it just wasn't important enough to make a big deal out of where I went to school." He wondered what she would think if he told her he'd never even wanted to be a lawyer. That was something else he'd never confided to anyone.

She didn't answer immediately, and he was afraid she thought he was a gutless wonder.

"I think what you're doing is good," she finally said.

He turned, gazing down into her eyes again. What he saw made him feel exactly the way he did when the Ferris wheel stopped at the very top of the ride and he looked down.

And in that moment, he knew he should have said goodbye to her when he'd intended to, because now it was too late.

"Eve! It's really you!"

Eve smiled. She would have known Jamie's voice anywhere. Twenty years of not hearing it hadn't made any difference at all. "Yes, it's really me."

"I wasn't sure you'd call," Jamie said.

"Why not?"

Eve could almost hear Jamie's shrug. "Well, it *has* been twenty years since I've heard from you."

"I know."

"I thought maybe you'd forgotten all about me."

"I could never forget you."

They were both silent for a long moment. Then Jamie said, "Eve, why did you just go away like that? I mean, I got home from Florida, and you were gone. Just like that. And you never answered my letters, and every time I called your brother's house, they said you were out. And you never called me back."

Eve nodded. "I know. I'm sorry. I...things were difficult for me just then."

"I thought maybe I'd done something wrong. I thought you were mad at me, or something." Jamie's voice trailed off uncertainly.

"No, I was never mad at you." Eve closed her eyes. As pleased as she was to hear Jamie's voice and as much as she wanted to see her old friend, was she ready to face these questions?

"I thought maybe you were ticked off about what happened that last night before I left for Florida. Remember? We went to the St. Ignatius Festival, but we met those two cute guys—remember?—Kevin McBride and Mitch Sinclair, and I kind of deserted you."

Eve swallowed. She'd hoped Jamie had forgotten about that night. "Oh, Jamie, don't be silly. I told you. I had some family problems, that's all."

Jamie sighed. "That's a relief. I really worried about that for a long time. Gosh, Eve, I've missed you. When can I see you? I'm dying to hear everything...get caught up on your life...gee, you're so famous. It must be wonderful." Jamie sounded wistful.

"And I'm anxious to hear about your life."

"Oh, me, I lead a boring life."

"But you're married and have children. I know you do, because my brother subscribes to the *Maple Hills Journal* and he's sent me clippings over the years. So your life can't be *too* boring."

"Compared to yours, it is."

Because she wanted to change the subject, Eve said, "Listen, will you be at the reception tomorrow night?"

Jamie laughed. "I don't exactly run in those circles."

"I thought things might have changed by now."

"Some things never change."

"How about tomorrow for lunch? Maybe you could come here to the inn."

"I'd love to."

They talked for a while longer, then agreed on a time for the following day and hung up. Afterward, Eve thought about their conversation. She was looking forward to seeing Jamie, but she hoped Jamie wouldn't question her too relentlessly. Especially not about Mitch Sinclair. Especially not about that night.

Friday, June third, twenty years earlier

Eve and Mitch talked for a long time, about everything. She told him about her brother and how he'd been hurt in Vietnam and she told him about how much she wanted to leave Maple Hills and see some of the places in the world she'd only read about.

He told her about his family and their expectations and how sometimes it was hard to live up to them. He told her about occasionally wishing he could just pack up his belongings and take off and forget about everything.

She could see that they were soul mates. The more he told her, the more she realized that underneath, he felt the same way she felt about so many things.

Before she knew it, it was nine-thirty and they'd been talking for more than an hour and a half. She couldn't believe how the time had flown. She had completely forgotten about Jamie until she saw Jamie and Kevin, holding hands and laughing, come walking across the grass to the picnic table where Eve and Mitch were sitting.

"We've been looking for you two all over!" Jamie said, eyes sparkling.

Kevin grinned, his dark eyes sliding from Mitch to Eve, then back to Mitch. "You two been hiding?" he said.

Eve suddenly felt self-conscious, even though she wasn't doing anything wrong.

"No," Mitch said mildly. "Just talking."

"Well, we wanted to tell you we're leaving," Jamie said.

Eve frowned. "Leaving?" Jamie knew Eve didn't like to walk home by herself late at night, especially not past Porter Woods.

"Yeah, Kevin and I are gonna go to a club he knows out on Route 36 near Delaware." Jamie's voice was laced with excitement.

Eve stared at Jamie. "But I thought we were going to go home together. Y-you're leaving for Florida tomorrow. I won't see you again for months."

"I'll call you from Florida," Jamie said. She grinned at Mitch. "If you don't want to go with us, Mitch'll take you home, won't you, Mitch?"

Mitch smiled at Eve. "I'll be glad to give you a ride home, Eve."

Eve knew her parents would be angry if they found out. One of their rules was she couldn't go out with a boy until they'd met him first. But getting a ride home with Mitch wasn't like a date, not really, so she wasn't breaking a rule. Was she?

Kevin winked. "Thanks, buddy."

Eve and Jamie hugged and said their goodbyes. Eve promised to write. And then Jamie and Kevin left.

After they were gone, Mitch said, "Do you want to leave, too? We could go for a ride. I've got a convertible, and we could put the top down."

It took Eve about two seconds to make up her mind. "Okay." She actually felt relieved, because she wanted to be with Mitch, but she didn't want anyone she knew to see her. What if one of her mother's Altar Society friends mentioned seeing the two of them together? Her mother would have a fit. Eve would get the third degree and a long lecture. Best to avoid all that if she could.

They drove out into the country. Eve loved Mitch's car—a cool, red Mustang. She loved the wind sailing through her hair. She loved the exhilarating sensation that she was free at last. But most of all, she loved being with Mitch. He was more than just the cutest boy she'd ever been around. He felt things deeply, just as she did, and he had suffered. When he'd talked about his brother dying and how he didn't want to hurt his parents because they'd been hurt so much already, Eve had melted inside. She'd wanted to put her arms around him and hold him close. She'd wanted to tell him how much she admired him.

As they rode along, Eve spun daydreams about him. It had been fate that they'd met tonight. He was the man she'd always imagined she would meet: strong and smart, handsome and sophisticated, yet sensitive and caring. And the fact that he was six years older was perfect, too. Boys her age were so immature and selfish.

They drove for about thirty minutes, then circled back, ending up on the west side of Porter Lake. Across the calm water, they could see the lights of the festival and Maple Hills in the distance.

Mitch cut the motor, but left the key turned on so that soft music played on the radio.

Her heart began to thump harder as he turned toward her, putting his right arm against the back of the seat.

Crickets sang, fireflies danced, and night creatures stirred in the woods surrounding them. The moon, full and bright, silvered the water.

"It's nice out here, isn't it?" Mitch said. His hand inched closer, his fingertips brushing her neck.

Eve shivered.

"Are you cold?"

"N-no," she said breathlessly.

His hand dropped to her shoulder. "You sure?"

She looked up at him. Her breathing quickened.

"Eve..."

His right arm slid around her, tugging her closer. His left hand touched her cheek.

She closed her eyes, her heart pounding.

Then he kissed her, and it was just like Eve had always imagined she'd feel when she met the right person. Fireworks went off in her head. He held her closer, his mouth slanting across hers, and the hand that had stroked her cheek slid up under her hair. He deepened the kiss, sliding his tongue into her mouth, and at the touch of his tongue, everything in Eve's body went haywire. Her blood rushed through her veins, her stomach coiled and tightened, her head spun, and something throbbed deep within.

The kiss went on and on.

Became two kisses.

Then three.

She wanted him to go on kissing her forever. She loved him. It was just like the movies. They'd taken one look and fallen in love, because he loved her, too. She just knew he did.

When his hand, trembling, moved slowly down to cup her right breast, Eve moaned as her nipples hardened. Mitch's kisses became greedier and more demanding as he brushed his hand back and forth against her nipples.

Mitch, Mitch.

Slowly he reached up under her hair and untied her halter top, baring her to her waist. She closed her eyes and reveled in the sensations skyrocketing through her body.

"Eve, oh, you're so beautiful," he said, his voice rough and shaky. He began to kiss her breasts, and when he took one of the nipples into his mouth, Eve thought she was going to die. She whimpered, but she pressed his head against her so he wouldn't stop.

Without even knowing how it had happened, she found herself lying across the seat. And then it was just Mitch's kisses and his hands touching, exploring, making her feel as if she were coming apart.

When he began to unbutton her skirt, she was only dimly aware of what was happening. Nothing mattered but the way she wanted him. Nothing mattered but the way they felt about each other. Nothing mattered but the knowledge that she'd been waiting all of her life for Mitch, and now he was here.

She clung to him. Her cries mingled with his as they joined together, awkwardly at first, then more surely. Happiness filled her heart, and she was so glad she *had* waited. She was so glad she hadn't been like a lot of the other girls—having sex with just any boy. This was so right, because Mitch was so wonderful.

It was only afterward, when he gently helped her get her clothes back on, that the realization of what she'd done, of what she'd let *him* do, actually hit her and she began to tremble.

Oh, God. Oh, God. Oh, God. She'd...she'd had sex with a boy she barely knew. With a boy she'd just met tonight!

Her mind raced.

Whirled.

What if her parents found out? They would kill her if they suspected what she'd done tonight. She hugged herself, her mind darting wildly. *Oh, God.* She couldn't look at Mitch. She could just imagine what he was thinking. Suddenly the enormity of her actions nearly overwhelmed her, and tears welled in her eyes.

"Oh, honey, don't. Don't cry. Please don't cry." He held her close, tucking her head under his chin. "It's okay."

She clung to him, crying harder. "Y-you probably think I'm . . . I'm ch-cheap," she sobbed.

"No, I don't. I think you're terrific."

"You're just saying that. I—I . . . don't even know you, and I, oh, God, I let you—"

His kiss stopped her mounting hysteria. He kissed her for a long time, whispering soothing words.

"You didn't *let* me do anything. We did something together. Something beautiful. I know what kind of girl you are. You're smart and pretty and nice and I liked you the first moment I saw you."

Finally she calmed down.

He gazed into her eyes, his expression tender. "This was your first time, wasn't it?" he whispered.

"Yes." She could feel his heart beating under her palm.

"I thought so." He stroked her hair. "I—I feel honored."

She swallowed. *Oh, Mitch, I love you. I'll always love you.*

He kissed her hair. "Please don't be sorry. I don't want you to be sorry."

She pulled back and searched his face. "You don't think I'm awful?"

"I told you. I think you're terrific." He kissed her tenderly, whispering against her mouth, "The nicest girl I've ever known."

Happiness flooded her, dispelling most of her panic, because she could hear the honesty in his voice. It was going to be okay. Because he really *did* think she was nice. "I—I think you're terrific, too," she said.

His kiss was sweet and gentle, just brushing her lips. They stayed at the lake for a long time.

Chapter Four

Eve returned the rest of her phone calls, then took a long, soothing bath and ordered a room service dinner. The strain of the day had taken its toll, and all she wanted was to go to bed early.

Unfortunately, her mind refused to turn off. Reliving the night she'd lost her virginity to Mitch had awakened all the buried emotions and unearthed all the old pain.

So she lay in bed and remembered the girl she was—the innocent who had gone home that night and spun daydreams around Mitchell Sinclair.

I was such a fool. I really thought he was the man of my dreams. That we'd get married and live happily ever after.

That first night, after Mitch took her home, she lay in her bed and hugged the soft white bunny he'd won for her. Over and over again, she replayed the events of the evening. How he told her he'd call her the next day. How he gave her one last, tender kiss and told her she was special, the most special girl he'd ever known.

How she believed him.

Those magical words dispelled all of her fears.

Then she hugged her bunny and fantasized about the future. She whispered, "I love you, Mitch. I love you." She was convinced he loved her. Of course, he did. He would have said so that night, but he probably thought it was too soon. After all, they'd only just met. They'd only spent the one night together.

She told herself the length of time they'd known each other didn't matter. She and Mitch were meant to be together. It was written in the stars. Their love was fated.

In her mind, she saw the way the rest of the summer would go. He would call her the next morning, and they would see each other again the following evening. And for the rest of the summer, they would be together every day.

Eve knew she'd have to work on her parents, but eventually they would meet Mitch, and they would approve. How could they not? He was so perfectly wonderful. So wonderfully perfect.

And when Mitch asked Eve to marry him, he would give her a beautiful diamond ring. She would show it to everyone. Her friends would all be so jealous. Shawn and Sarah Nicholls would be bug-eyed when they found out. The ladies in her mother's Altar Society would be bug-eyed, too.

Mitchell Sinclair.

Eve sighed dreamily.

"Mrs. Mitchell Sinclair." She tested the words on her tongue as she whispered them aloud. "Eve Sinclair."

It had taken her a long time to fall asleep that night, and even now, so many years later, she remembered that when she finally did, she had been so happy and so absolutely certain that only wonderful things were in store for her.

Eve bit her bottom lip.

Oh, God, she'd been so stupid! So naive! She had really believed that what she and Mitch had shared was special. That it was important to him—that it wasn't just sex with a willing girl—that he had recognized the inevitability of their meeting. She had honestly thought that they were meant to be together forever.

She grimaced. The old pain pushed its way up from the dark recesses of her soul. Fighting it, angry at herself, she punched up her pillow and buried her head.

She had thought she could handle the memories. She had thought her only emotions would be gratitude that she'd escaped the confines of a small-town marriage and a small-town mentality. She had expected to feel amusement and satisfaction. She had imagined herself laughing at the way the townspeople would worship at her feet.

She told herself to get a grip.

She fell asleep determined that for the rest of her stay in Maple Hills, she would remember who she was and not who she had been.

"I would have known you anywhere," Eve said.

"You, too," said Jamie.

After a few awkward moments when Jamie had first arrived, the two women had hugged tightly, and now, seated at their corner table overlooking the inn's renowned rose garden, they had settled into a comfortable conversation.

Eve thought Jamie looked wonderful. The round-ness of her adolescence, which could have gone the other way, had disappeared, and Jamie's five-foot-eight-inch frame was lean and firm. Her brown hair was short and frosted, and her dark eyes were still lively and curious. And she was wearing an Eve DelVecchio dress—one of last year's most popular designs—a lemon yellow with softly pleated skirt from Eden's Forbidden Fruit collection.

"I like your taste in clothes," Eve said.

Jamie laughed. "I just wish I could afford to buy more of your designs. They're fantastic."

"Thanks."

Jamie's smile softened. "I'm so proud of you, Eve. You've really made a success of your life."

Eve nodded. She never disparaged her accomplish-ments or dismissed people's compliments. She had worked too hard for her success.

"I envy you, you know," Jamie added. "I used to daydream about becoming an actress. But I never had the guts to do anything about it."

"But you're married, and you have...what?—three children?"

Jamie nodded. "Yeah." Her eyes lit up again. "And guess what? My oldest—Rachel? She's going to be a senior this year, and colleges like Princeton and Brown are already after her."

"Wow! That's great. She must be smart."

"She is," Jamie said proudly. "And not only smart, but gorgeous."

"Have you got pictures?"

"Have I got pictures!" Jamie reached down for her purse and extracted a slim wallet.

Eve tried to ignore the pang of envy that pricked her as she studied the photo of the beautiful girl. She'd never been able to play the proud mother. Never been able to show pictures of a beloved child. She wondered if Jamie knew how truly lucky she was. Eve would have sold her soul for the right to brag as only a mother could. "She *is* gorgeous, Jamie," she said softly.

"And that's Robert," Jamie said, reaching over to flip to another picture. "He's fourteen."

A good-looking boy with Jamie's eyes grinned out at Eve. The pang became a sharp ache in the vicinity of Eve's heart.

"And that's Renee, our baby. She's ten."

"They're great kids," Eve said.

"Yeah, they are."

The two women stopped talking as their waiter served them—a vegetable stir-fry for Jamie and a grilled chicken salad for Eve.

Once the waiter left, Eve said, "And you married Bob Zimmerman. I never would've put the two of you together."

Jamie laughed. "I know. That's what everyone says, especially Bob's mother." She rolled her eyes. "She, of course, planned for her only chick to marry some intellectual who would help her perfect son produce perfect children. She nearly had a cow when he announced he wanted to marry me. She's something else. Do you remember her?"

Eve grinned. Who could forget Maida Zimmerman? She was an institution in Maple Hills. She'd been the head librarian at the Maple Hills Public Library ever since Eve could remember. She hadn't married until she was in her mid forties, and then she'd astounded everyone by having a baby the following year. "Of course, I remember her. Is she still alive?"

"Yeah, she's still alive. She's ninety-one and still as sharp as a tack. With a tongue to match," Jamie said dryly.

"You poor thing."

Jamie chuckled. "Oh, it's not so bad. She's not so bad. She adores the kids and when she was younger, she never minded baby-sitting. I just ignore her little jabs at me. I figure that's one of the privileges of growing old— getting to say what you think."

"You really *haven't* changed. You still always manage to find a bright side to everything."

Jamie shrugged. "Shoot, why not?" She took a bite of her food and chewed thoughtfully. "What's the point in constantly moaning about things you can't change? Bob's mother is Bob's mother. I can't change her, and it's a waste of energy to bitch all the time."

Yes, Eve had learned that lesson, too.

"But let's talk about you for a change," Jamie said. "I want to hear everything. Start with why you left Maple Hills the way you did."

"Look, Jamie, if you don't mind, I really would rather not. It was a family thing, and it's over now, and I don't like to think about it." She held her breath. *Please, Jamie, don't push it.*

Jamie studied her for a moment. "Okay. Start wherever you like, then."

Eve released her breath slowly. It was going to be all right. Jamie wasn't going to press her. "Well, I lived with my brother and helped my sister-in-law for about a year. She and my brother had adopted a baby, and Mary Ann really needed help."

Jamie smiled. "Gee, that's great they were able to adopt. I know you used to talk about how much they wanted a baby, especially your brother."

Eve nodded. "Yes, they were thrilled. Anyway, I stayed with them until Matthew was a year old, and Mary Ann finally felt like she could manage on her own. It was probably a good thing, too, because I was getting awfully attached to Matthew myself. Anyway, Tony paid my way to a design school in New York. For the next two years, I went to school full-time and stayed in the city during the week then went to Connecticut on the weekends. When I graduated, I was offered an apprenticeship with Jonathan Douglas. I worked for him for four years, then decided to strike out on my own, and well..."

"The rest is history...." Jamie said.

"Yes."

"What about your personal life? I read about you and that Scotch businessman. I thought maybe you were going to marry him."

Eve smiled. She had met Colin McDermott on one of her many trips abroad. He was a very successful and attractive man, and she had dated him off and on for several years. For some reason, the gossip columns had played up their involvement and speculated about a possible marriage. "Our lives were too far apart for marriage. Colin would never have been happy in the States, and I had no interest in moving to Scotland. We're still friends, though."

"And there's never been anyone else?"

"No, nobody serious." Unbidden, Mitch's face flickered through her mind. She struggled not to let her own face betray the unwelcome reminder that once

there had been someone—someone very important—
and that he was still impacting her life.

"Well, marriage isn't for everybody," Jamie said
philosophically. "You're probably better off. You've
got enough money to do whatever you want to do, and
I'll bet you never lack for someone to do things with."

"No, I don't lack for companionship."

"What about kids, though?" Jamie said. "Have you
ever thought about having a child?"

Eve swallowed. This was a painful subject, one she
would have preferred not to discuss. "At one time, it's
about the only thing I *did* think about," she finally said.

"And now?"

Eve slowly smiled. "Now I channel all my motherly
instincts into spoiling Matthew."

"Matthew? Oh, your brother's child."

Eve nodded and ate some of her salad. She'd had
enough of talking about marriage and children. It was
a subject she usually tried to steer clear of, and after
today, she knew she'd been right to avoid it.

Who needed reminders of all she'd missed?

Eve would rather focus on all she had. After all, she
had more than most women ever dreamed of having.

She smiled brightly at Jamie. "Tell me about Shawn
and Sarah Nicholls and the rest of the old gang. I'm
dying to get caught up on all the news."

The phone rang just as Mitch opened the back door.
He debated ignoring the call. He didn't want to be late
for the reception. But the thought that it might be
Nicholas stopped him. He turned around and reached
for the portable phone sitting on a nearby counter.

"Hello?"

"Dad?"

It *was* Nicholas. Mitch grinned. "Hey, sport, what're you doing up so late?" It was almost one o'clock in the morning in London.

"Oh, Granddad and Grandma took me to the theater, and then we went out for a late supper, and we just got back to the hotel, so I thought I'd see if you were home."

"I almost wasn't," Mitch said. He was still smiling. Although his marriage to Carolyn had been a disaster from the beginning, Nicholas's birth had made up for a lot. And since Carolyn's death when Nicholas was eight, Mitch and his son had grown very close. "I was just leaving for a reception at the country club."

"What kind of reception?" Nicholas asked.

"It's a party being given for a famous fashion designer who used to live here in Maple Hills."

"That oughta be fun. You taking a date?"

Mitch pulled out one of the kitchen chairs and straddled it. He grinned. Since Nicholas had become interested in girls himself, he seemed to have taken an inordinate interest in Mitch's social life. "No. No date."

"Dad, you know, it'd be good for you if—"

"Hey, let's not waste time and your grandparents' money talking about me," Mitch said, interrupting Nicholas firmly. "Tell me what you're doing. You still having fun?"

"Yeah. We're havin' a great time."

"So what have you seen so far?"

Nicholas gave him a complete rundown on Buckingham Palace, the changing of the palace guard, Piccadilly Circus, the double-decker buses, and their hotel. "Tomorrow we're taking the train to Stratford-upon-Avon."

"You'll enjoy that."

"I'm looking forward to it because Grandma says it was Mom's favorite place to visit."

Mitch refrained from contradicting Joanna Whittaker's romanticized view of her daughter, but Mitch knew Carolyn much preferred places like Harrods and London's theater district to the home of the Bard.

He and Nicholas talked for a few more minutes, then Mitch looked up at the wall clock and saw that if he didn't get out of there in the next two minutes, he *would* be late. He frowned. He really wanted to be at the reception when Eve arrived. "Listen, Nicholas, I'm sorry, but I've got to get going. The reception's supposed to start in thirty minutes."

"That's okay, Dad. I'll call you when we get to Paris."

They said their goodbyes, and Mitch hurried out to his car. He drove faster than usual and made it to the Maple Hills Country Club with ten minutes to spare.

As he made his way inside, heading toward the upstairs ballroom where the reception was being held, he was greeted by dozens of friends and acquaintances, most of them on their way to the reception, too.

"Hey, Mitch, missed you today," said Kevin McBride, who walked out of the bar just as Mitch passed the entrance.

"Yeah, well, it couldn't be helped. How'd you do?"

Kevin grinned. "Shot a seventy-eight on the front nine and an eighty-two on the back nine."

Mitch chuckled. "Who was keeping score? You?"

Kevin gave him a playful punch. "Ned Falkoff was keeping score, and you know damn well he'd add a few strokes if he could."

The two men continued to talk about the morning's golf game as they climbed the stairs together. Then Kevin said, "I wonder what she'll be like now?"

"Who?" Mitch said, playing dumb.

Kevin gave him a quizzical look. "The famous Eve DelVecchio. Who else?"

Mitch shrugged. "We'll soon see."

"You dated her a couple of times, didn't you?"

Even though Mitch had been prepared for the possibility of Kevin's remembering that night so long ago, his heart still gave an unwelcome lurch. He had never told anyone about his relationship with Eve. It would not have been fair to either her or Carolyn. The lie came smoothly to his lips. "No, not really."

Kevin frowned. "But I thought—" He broke off as Candy Barnwell, a striking blonde dressed in a clinging red slip dress, waved to him. "There's Candy." He winked. "See you later."

Mitch was glad to see Kevin go. Although the two men had been friends ever since high school, a little of the adult Kevin went a long way. Married and divorced three times, he never tired of boasting about his sexual exploits, a subject that did not interest Mitch at all. Mitch wondered if the women with whom Kevin had had affairs knew how much he talked. Or if they even cared.

Mitch slowly made his way into the crowded ballroom. It looked as if all the movers and shakers were there—a couple of hundred people at the very least. He spied Terry Flynn and his wife near the bandstand and walked in their direction.

"Hi, Mitch."

"Hello, Mitch."

"Good to see you, Mitch."

Mitch returned the greetings, smiling and shaking hands and complimenting the women.

When he reached Terry Flynn's group, he stood quietly on the fringes and waited until Terry noticed him. "Mitch!" Terry finally said. "Glad you made it. The guest of honor should be here any minute. I sent a car over to the inn to pick her up."

Mitch nodded, smiled at Ann Marie, Terry's wife, and answered a question put to him by her twin sister, Alana. All the while he kept one eye on the big double doors and tried to quell the unsettled feeling in the pit of his stomach. He told himself he was being ridiculous, acting like a green kid on a first date.

She probably won't even remember you.

The thought stung, even though Mitch knew it would be better for both of them if their long-ago relationship had been relegated to the status of a high school crush and nothing more.

"Have you talked to Nicholas? Is he enjoying his trip?" Ann Marie Flynn asked, her warm brown eyes shining softly.

"Talked to him tonight," Mitch said. He returned her smile. He liked Ann Marie. She was completely unpretentious.

"Shannon sure misses him." The Flynns' oldest daughter and Nicholas had been inseparable throughout their freshman year. "But I think it's good that they're spending some time apart."

Mitch agreed. Nicholas and Shannon were both too young for that kind of involvement.

Just then an excited murmur rippled through the crowd, and Mitch knew without being told that the object of his own youthful romance had arrived.

He turned around slowly.

Eve stood on the threshold of the large room. For just a few moments, no one realized she was there, and she took advantage of the brief respite before the inevitable storm of greetings began.

She had dressed carefully tonight. She wanted to look spectacular. She wanted the women to be envious of her looks and her jewelry and clothing, and she wanted the men to speculate on what she'd be like in bed.

Most of all, she wanted Mitch Sinclair to realize exactly what he'd thrown away when he'd chosen someone else instead of her.

She knew she had achieved the effect she desired. The strapless white crepe evening dress was one of her most sophisticated designs. She especially loved the skirt, which was narrow, with a long slit skirt that showed a tantalizing amount of leg every time she moved.

Her heart beat a little faster. Was Mitch here tonight? Was he even now watching her?

She raised her chin a notch and took a deep breath. The breeze drifting in from the open French doors felt good against her bare shoulders.

She knew exactly when the first person spotted her. An excited buzz raced through the room, and within seconds, she was surrounded.

"Miss DelVecchio, welcome to Maple Hills!" gushed a willowy woman with salt-and-pepper hair. "I'm Joan Castleman, I used to be Joan Perry...we lived on Wilson Avenue...my mother and your mother were in the Altar Society together...."

Eve smiled and shook the woman's hand. "Of course," she said politely, although she didn't remember Joan Castleman or her mother.

"Miss DelVecchio, hello," said a short, plump woman in her fifties. "You probably don't remember me...Cathie Andrews...from the market...."

"Hi. Good to see you again."

Dozens of others said hello, introducing themselves and shaking her hand and complimenting her on her appearance. Eve smiled graciously and gave each of them her full attention for a few seconds. She was still standing in the doorway.

Then a tall, dark-haired man accompanied by a sweet-looking woman approached, and the crowd parted to let them pass.

"Miss DelVecchio," he said, smiling widely. "I'm Terry Flynn." He reached for her hand, shaking it firmly. "It's very nice to meet you, and welcome home to Maple Hills."

"Thank you. It's very nice to be here. And I appreciate you sending the car for me."

"My pleasure." He drew the woman at his side forward. "I'd like you to meet my wife, Ann Marie."

"Hello." Ann Marie Flynn smiled, her eyes friendly.

Eve warmed to the mayor's wife immediately.

They talked for a few minutes, then Terry and Ann Marie led Eve through the throng to a table near the front of the room. Dozens of people milled around it, and soon Eve was engulfed in more introductions and yet more compliments.

Through it all, her body hummed with tension and anticipation. She knew it was only a matter of moments before she would see Mitch again. It took all of her concentration and considerable self-discipline to keep her eyes from scanning the room.

Then, just as she began to think she might have been wrong—maybe he *hadn't* been invited tonight—she felt a light touch on her upper arm.

She turned.

Looked up.

And for one long moment couldn't breathe.

His eyes were just as she remembered them. Brown flecked with gold.

Everyone else faded from her consciousness.

"Hello, Eve."

His voice was just as she remembered it, too. Deep, rich, still capable of sending goose bumps up her arms.

"Hello, Mitch."

"Oh, you two know each other!" Ann Marie's voice said. "You didn't tell me you knew her, Mitch."

Eve felt trapped by her inability to tear her gaze from his. She wanted to say something light and sophisticated, something that said, *Don't think I'm all aflutter over seeing you again, because I'm not. You mean nothing to me. Nothing.* But the only thing that came out of her mouth was, "How have you been?" and even then, the words sounded strained and stilted, as if she'd had to pull them out of her throat.

He smiled then, that devastating smile that could melt even the coldest heart, and Eve knew it wasn't going to be quite as easy as she'd imagined to act indifferent to him.

Because, unfortunately for her, the years had been very kind to him. He was, if anything, even better looking than he'd been as a young man.

It was frustrating to admit it, but she was still attracted to him.

Still, no matter how hard it was, she would never, ever, let him know it.

Chapter Five

Mitch felt as if someone had taken a pole and rammed it into his gut. His senses reeled, and it took every bit of willpower he possessed to keep his voice steady and his expression from betraying how completely stunned he was by his first sight of Eve in the flesh.

All these years of thinking about her, of remembering her, simply hadn't prepared him for the emotions that now pummeled him.

She was breathtaking.

Heart-stoppingly beautiful.

In fact, he couldn't believe how beautiful. He'd seen pictures of her over the years, but they hadn't done her justice.

Everything about her—from the top of her shining hair to the tips of her toes—was sleek perfection.

And those eyes.

They had always mesmerized him, but they were even more mesmerizing now that she knew how to enhance their size and hazy color with the subtle use of makeup and clothing.

"I've been fine," he finally answered. "I guess I don't have to ask about you, do I? The whole town is proud of your success."

She smiled politely. "Thank you."

Mitch fought his feelings of awkwardness. He knew there were dozens of curious eyes upon them. He would act natural if it killed him. "My mother is very excited at the prospect of entertaining you Sunday," he said. He wondered what Eve was thinking as she returned his gaze evenly.

"I'm looking forward to meeting her." Her expression gave away nothing.

As Mitch searched for something else to say, the band began to play, and impulsively he said, "Would you like to dance?"

For just a moment, her calm veneer showed a tiny crack as some unidentifiable emotion flickered in her eyes, but she quickly masked it. Again her smile was polite. "Thank you. Perhaps later."

"Of course." He smiled, too, then turned away, determined not to let her see that her refusal had stung. Had it been a deliberate attempt to set him in his place and show him how totally insignificant he was in her life?

He hoped not. He hoped she'd long ago gotten over the hurt he'd caused her. Once again, as it had so many times over the years, deep regret coursed through him for what might have been.

For the next hour, he watched her surreptitiously. As she talked and smiled, constantly surrounded by ad-

miring guests, he slowly realized that the changes in her
went far deeper than her surface appearance. Gone was
the wide-eyed innocence, the warmth and sweet open-
ness that had so appealed to him. Now her expression,
her entire demeanor, while gracious and pleasant, was
coolly elegant and reserved, perhaps even cautious.

This new Eve would not act impulsively or emotion-
ally as she had when she was young. This Eve sat back,
watched, waited, observed. She would think carefully
before she did or said anything.

The changes saddened Mitch and deepened his regret, even though he knew it was ridiculous to have expected anything else. After all, Eve was no longer a
naive seventeen-year-old. She was a grown woman—
worldly, successful, rich, famous. If he had entertained the fantasy that she would still be the same, *he*
was the one who was naive!

He wondered if his treatment of her had anything to
do with the way she was now. Then he told himself not
to attach so much importance to his role in her life. After all, twenty years had passed. Of course, she was
different. Hell, so was he.

*What did you think? That you could recapture your
youth? Make up for your mistakes? Somehow erase the
past twenty years? Did you think she would fall into
your arms again?*

He sighed wearily. God! He was an idiot. That's exactly what he'd thought, even though he'd never admitted it until this moment. What was wrong with him?
Eve was an entirely different person than she'd been
when he knew her. She had probably long dismissed
what had happened between them. She had probably
had dozens of lovers in the intervening years. Her refusal to dance with him had probably had no signifi-

cance at all beyond the fact that she just hadn't felt like dancing, with him or anyone else.

Go home. He knew he should. There was no point in him staying. He'd seen her. They'd talked. She remembered him, but she was not the least bit interested in renewing any kind of relationship, even that of friends.

Although he told himself this, he couldn't seem to act on his advice.

"She's beautiful, isn't she?"

Mitch jumped guiltily. He smiled down at Ann Marie, who had walked up to him so quietly he hadn't been aware of her presence until she spoke. "Yes, very."

"I was really surprised to see that you knew her. You never mentioned her."

Mitch wished Ann Marie's brown eyes weren't quite so astute. "We were kids when we met. I wasn't even sure she remembered me."

Ann Marie nodded, her gaze once again resting on Eve, who had just walked onto the dance floor with Terry.

"Aren't you jealous?" Mitch said lightly. *I am.* He couldn't seem to tear his gaze away from Eve and the mayor.

Ann Marie smiled. "No, but I sure would like to dance, too."

Mitch smiled and bowed slightly. He held out his hand. "Your wish is my command."

Moments later, as he and Ann Marie circled close to Terry and Eve, Mitch gave way to a second impulsive gesture. "Shall we exchange partners for a while?" he said to Terry.

Since Terry could hardly refuse, he relinquished Eve, and as Mitch took her into his arms, his gaze met Ann

Marie's for a brief moment. Hers was thoughtful. He hoped his was noncommittal.

And then his entire attention was focused on Eve. "I hope you don't mind," he said.

She looked up. "Of course not." Her tone was guarded.

Suddenly Mitch couldn't stand her aloofness, this pretense that they were nothing more than old acquaintances. Fair or not, he wanted to see some reaction from her. He wanted to know that she *remembered,* dammit! "I wouldn't blame you if you did mind."

She stiffened only slightly, but it was enough to show him that she wasn't quite as detached as she would have him believe.

"I've always regretted the way things ended up between us," he said, determined to get it all out in the open once and for all. He took a deep breath. "I'm sorry I hurt you."

She shrugged. "Don't give it another thought." She smiled, but for just a millisecond, pain clouded her eyes, then her protective mask clicked into place and the emotion was hidden. "We were very young."

If Mitch hadn't glimpsed that pain, he might have been forced to concede defeat. But he had, and a tiny sliver of hope gave him the impetus to press on. "I've never forgotten you," he said softly.

He felt the almost imperceptible shudder that raced through her. *She remembers, too,* he thought triumphantly. *She's not nearly as indifferent as she pretends to be.*

"I rarely think about the past," she said.

He knew she was lying, even though her expression was once again shuttered. "I spend too much time thinking about it," he said honestly. He could feel the warmth of her skin through the thin material of her dress. He could see the little pulse that beat in the hollow of her throat. He could smell the fragrance of her hair and the richness of her expensive perfume. And even though his emotions were turbulent, he felt oddly elated, because for the first time in many years, all his senses were alive. He knew that even if she totally rebuffed him, he would continue trying to get past the wall she'd erected between them.

Her gaze met his. For a long moment, they looked into each other's eyes. "Where is your wife tonight?" she finally said.

"My wife died seven years ago."

"Oh. I—I'm sorry to hear that."

He nodded. "Thank you." Then because he would have wanted to know if he'd been in her shoes, he added, "It was an accident. She had been having migraine headaches and a lot of trouble sleeping. Anyway, she took an overdose of sleeping pills."

"Oh, Mitch..."

The way she said his name, the genuine sympathy he saw in her eyes, encouraged him to continue. "I've always felt guilty, because I know she wasn't happy." It was the first time he'd ever admitted his guilty feelings to anyone, and it felt wonderful. It had always been this way with Eve. Even that first night together he'd told her his innermost secrets and shared emotions and thoughts never before shared with another person. It made him feel good to discover the connection between them still existed, whether Eve realized it or not.

"You shouldn't feel guilty," she continued. "People aren't responsible for the happiness of others." Her smile was wry. "I learned that a long time ago."

Mitch wished they weren't surrounded by so many people. There were so many things he wanted to say.

"But you're not alone," she continued. "You have a child . . . or is it children?"

Thinking of Nicholas always brought a smile to Mitch's face. "It's *child*. We had one son . . . Nicholas. He's fifteen."

She frowned. "Fifteen? But I thought—" She broke off abruptly.

Mitch knew what she'd thought, but now was not the time, nor was this the place, to explain. "You know, it's funny, but I always wanted a whole slew of kids. I guess losing my brother the way I did, I hated for anyone to grow up as an only child. But it didn't work out that way. Still, if one kid is all I'm ever going to have, I'm lucky to have a kid as terrific as Nicholas."

Something, some unnamed emotion, momentarily clouded her eyes, and Mitch immediately felt like kicking himself. He should have known better than to whine about only having one child when Eve had none. But if his comments had bothered her, she pulled herself together quickly and said, "It's easy to see you're proud of him."

He smiled. "Yes, I am, but we've talked about me long enough. What about you?"

"There's nothing to tell," she said quickly. "My life's an open book. Work . . . and more work."

No one's life was an open book. Mitch had learned *that* a long time ago.

Just then, the song ended, and it was time to relinquish her to others. Already Mitch saw several people heading their way. He wished he could keep her to himself, but he knew it was a futile wish. Reluctantly he said, "Thank you for the dance. I enjoyed talking to you."

She nodded, not quite meeting his eyes. "Yes, it was nice getting caught up."

As he walked away, he wondered if she felt half as battered as he did.

Eve hoped the rest of the evening would pass quickly. She wanted nothing so much as to go back to the inn, where she could think about Mitch and their conversation in the privacy of her room.

She tried hard to keep her thoughts at bay, but her mind whirled even as she said polite nothings to dozens of dance partners, even as she smiled and laughed and pretended to be having a wonderful time.

Carolyn Sinclair was dead. She had died from an accidental overdose of sleeping pills. She had been unhappy. And so had Mitch. He hadn't even attempted to disguise his feelings when he'd told Eve about his wife.

And their son was only fifteen.

What had happened?

What had happened to the baby Carolyn was carrying twenty years ago?

Had everything Mitch told her that last terrible night been a lie?

As her thoughts tumbled, Eve forced herself not to look in Mitch's direction. She knew exactly where he was. He was standing on the other side of the big room, and the few times she'd glanced that way, he'd been watching her. Her heart had skidded, and she knew her calm facade was in danger of crumbling if she wasn't careful.

She thought the speeches would never end. She smiled so much her face began to ache.

Finally the evening was over. Finally she could say goodbye to everyone and make her escape. She geared herself for the one last hurdle of saying good-night to Mitch.

She was lucky.

When he approached her, she was in the midst of a dozen other people, and all he had a chance to say was, "Good night, Eve. It was really nice seeing you again."

"Yes. Good night." She gave him a practiced smile, then hurriedly looked away.

Ten minutes later she was sitting in the back seat of the limo and on her way to the inn. And twenty minutes after that, she was in the elevator and on her way to her suite. At exactly midnight, she walked inside.

And finally, she was able to give free rein to her emotions. She kicked off her pumps and sank down onto the sofa, leaned her head back, closed her eyes and allowed all the memories to come.

June, twenty years earlier

The weeks after the festival were exactly the way Eve had imagined they would be.

She saw Mitch every day. She got very creative in what she told her mother, especially since Jamie was away for the summer. Still, it wasn't difficult to deceive Angela, because Eve had never before done so, and her mother had no reason to think she would now.

She told her mother she was going to the library to research fashion design, or she said she was meeting the gang at the community center or a softball game or the movies, and instead she would sneak off to the edge of Porter Woods, where Mitch would pick her up. Then they would head off to their favorite spot at the lake, where they would talk and laugh and make love for hours. Or they would ride around, top down, wind flying through their hair, to places deep in the country.

They went for walks in meadows and made love in the tall grass.

They went to movies in nearby towns where no one knew them, sitting way back in the darkest corners where they held hands and kissed until their bodies cried out for more. Then, filled with unbearable excitement, they would leave and find a place where they could touch each other and light that fiery passion that consumed them.

Once they even rented a motel room about sixty miles north of Maple Hills. That was the only time that Eve felt vaguely dirty, but the feeling passed quickly because it was such a pleasure to get entirely naked together and make love on a soft bed and clean sheets.

And afterward. Oh, afterward had been wonderful. Eve blushed every time she thought about afterward when they'd soaped each other in the shower and Mitch had shown her a different way to make love.

They were always careful to get Eve home well before curfew so as to never give her parents reason to check up on her. Occasionally Eve felt guilty about deceiving her parents, but the feeling didn't last long. She was too deep in the throes of newly awakened passions and young love.

The weeks passed in a joyous blur. The days were shining and golden—filled with a delicious anticipation and excitement. The nights were trembling and mysterious—filled with dark delight.

But all too soon it was the last week of July. Before long, Mitch would have to go back to school. Eve couldn't bear to think about him leaving. Her own college prospects didn't excite her at all anymore—not since meeting Mitch. How would she survive until he could come back home? If only he went to school somewhere closer and could come home on the weekends. She wondered if she dared broach the subject. She wondered if he would consider transferring from Yale.

Then, on Wednesday night of that last week of the month, the subject came out into the open. Eve knew something was in the wind, even before Mitch said anything, because he seemed preoccupied as they drove along the country roads.

When he pulled into their place at the lake and turned off the ignition, the quiet of the night settled around them. He put his arm around her and drew her close. She lifted her face for his kiss, and when his lips covered hers, she sighed.

He kissed her gently, and when she reached up to twine her arms around his neck, he said, "Wait, Eve...there's, there's something we have to talk about."

She saw him swallow, his Adam's apple bobbing in his throat, and she felt oddly motherly toward him. She knew he was nervous, and she thought she knew why. He was finally going to tell her how he felt about her.

Happiness flooded her. "All right," she said softly. *Don't worry, Mitch. I love you, too. It's going to be fine. Don't be nervous.* She willed him to know her thoughts by giving his hand an encouraging squeeze.

He cleared his throat.

He *was* nervous! She smiled up at him. His eyes, always so warm and friendly and open, were engulfed in shadows.

"Eve, I...there's something I should have told you a long time ago."

Eve's heart lifted. *Say it. Don't be afraid.*

"I have no excuse for not telling you, just that there never seemed to be a right time. . . ." He sighed heavily. And then he used a four-letter word.

Slowly, something very like fear crept along Eve's spine. Mitch never used bad language, especially not that word. That was one of the things she liked so much about him, the way he showed his respect for her. She swallowed. Was something wrong?

"Eve . . ." His voice sounded strained. "When I met you, I already had a girlfriend. I—I *do* have a girlfriend."

Eve recoiled. She felt as if he'd hit her. She wet her lips. "I—I don't believe you," she whispered. "How . . . how could you spend so much time with me if you . . . if you . . . already have a girlfriend?"

"She's been away. In Europe."

"She's been away," Eve repeated woodenly. "Does . . . does that mean she's home now?" Now the fear consumed her, pressing against her chest like a slab of concrete. It was hard to breathe.

"She's coming home tomorrow."

How could he say it so matter-of-factly? her mind cried. How could he sit there and say those awful words as if he were telling her it was going to rain tomorrow? Didn't he know he was killing her? Didn't he love her? What had they been doing these past weeks, if he didn't love her? *Oh, God. Please, God.*

His arms tightened around her. He pressed his face against her hair. His hands trembled as they stroked her cheek. "I'm sorry, Eve. I should have told you. I know that."

What did this mean? It was all she could think. She wished she had the courage to voice the question, but she was afraid of the answer.

He lifted her chin, kissing her greedily. Eve's head spun as his tongue plunged into her mouth. He held her tightly and kissed her for a long time. Then, slowly, breathing hard, he released her. "I love you," he said raggedly. "I love you, and somehow, I'll make things right."

He loved her! He'd finally said he loved her, the words she'd been waiting to hear for weeks. Yet the unbridled joy she should have felt was spoiled by the pain his revelation had wrought. "Who...who is she?" Eve finally managed to ask.

And so he told her. Eve listened, her mind churning. She was Carolyn Whittaker, the daughter of old family friends. She had been engaged to his older brother, Cliff, and when Cliff died, she and Mitch had gradually drifted into a relationship.

"She took the European trip with her parents. They go every year. She's been gone since early in the summer." He grimaced. "She left the night before I met you."

Eve's heart was pounding so hard it scared her. "H-how do you feel about her?"

He sighed. "I care for her. She's a nice person, but I don't love her. I'm not *in* love with her." He stroked Eve's cheek, his touch familiar, warm, safe. "She's never made me feel the way you make me feel," he murmured. "I love you so much."

Something warm and wonderful shimmered through Eve. "Mitch," she whispered back, "I love you, too."

They kissed again. And again.

Carolyn Whittaker wasn't important, Eve told herself. He didn't love her. He loved Eve. That was all that mattered.

"I knew before Carolyn left," Mitch continued when they finally broke apart, "that I'd have to tell her how I really felt. I knew I couldn't marry her the way our parents expected. But I didn't want to spoil her trip, so I decided I'd wait until she got home."

Eve shivered.

His arms tightened around her. "Don't worry, Eve. It's going to be all right. I promise you," Mitch said. "Will you give me a few days to get things straightened out?" He tunneled his hands through her hair and kissed her lips gently. "I'll tell her first. I owe her that much. Then I'll talk to my parents. Okay?"

"Okay," Eve whispered.

"We'll meet Saturday night in our usual place."

"Yes."

And then they made love, sweetly and slowly, sealing their promises to each other with each kiss and each tender touch. And when Mitch finally dropped Eve off a block away from her apartment, the last thing he said was, "I love you. I'll see you on Saturday."

"Saturday."

In just two days, Eve's dreams would all come true.

As Mitch drove home from the reception, he couldn't stop thinking about the past. He fought against it. He hated remembering his mistakes and failures. It was counterproductive, because he couldn't change anything that had happened.

Uppermost in his thoughts, the scene he replayed again and again, was when he'd told Carolyn about Eve.

He had been apprehensive but determined, that long-ago Thursday morning at breakfast. Because of that, he had been quieter than usual. Even his mother had noticed.

"You're awfully quiet this morning," she said.

Mitch looked up from his cereal.

She eyed him thoughtfully as she buttered a blueberry muffin. "You shouldn't stay out so late."

He made a noncommittal sound and resumed eating.

"Where did you go last night?" she persisted. "Out with Kevin again?"

He swallowed. "Oh, just hangin' around. You know." He willed her to stop quizzing him.

"But *where* do you boys hang around?"

"Pamela," Mitch's father said, glancing up from his newspaper, "Mitch is twenty-three years old, in case you've forgotten. He doesn't have to tell you his every movement or his every thought."

Her face stiffened, and she gave his father a dirty look. "Mitch doesn't mind my questions, do you, Mitch?" she said.

Mitch's father rolled his eyes and turned his attention back to the paper.

Mitch decided it was safest not to answer. He hated being put in a position where he was forced to lie to her. He began to eat his cereal again. He had enough on his mind this morning without her third degree.

A few moments passed, and he thought he was out of the woods. Then she said, "Oh, I know why you seem so preoccupied! Today's the day Carolyn comes home! You probably can't wait to see her."

Mitch didn't look up immediately. What kind of answer could he give her?

His mother smiled. Her gaze was soft as it met his. "It's okay. I know how you feel."

Guilt slid through Mitch. He wondered what his mother would say if she knew what had happened to him over the past weeks. The weight of his deception hung heavy on his shoulders. For a brief moment, he was tempted to just blurt out the truth, say something like, *Mom, I don't love Carolyn and I don't want to marry her. I'm going to tell her that the minute I see her. I knew I had to even before I went to the festival last month, but after meeting this girl...*

He broke off the thought abruptly. What was he thinking of? No way he could say that to his mother. She'd flip out.

Besides, he owed it to Carolyn not to discuss his feelings about her with anyone else before talking to her. It was bad enough that he'd gotten involved with Eve behind Carolyn's back.

And as much as he was dreading the coming confrontation, he realized his mother was right. Although it would be hard to tell Carolyn they had no future together, it would be a relief to finally get his feelings out in the open.

Chapter Six

"What do you mean, you've met someone else?"

Mitch cringed at the shrill note in Carolyn's voice. He wished he could disappear, but he knew he deserved whatever she cared to dish out. "I'm sorry," he said inadequately.

She glared at him, her blue eyes narrowed into two furious slits. She made a visible effort to calm herself, and when she spoke again, her voice was clipped. "We're engaged, in case you've forgotten."

"Carolyn, you..." Mitch sighed. His voice was gentle as he continued. "You know we're not *really* engaged. I do realize that you assumed, that everyone has assumed—"

"How can you say that?" she shouted. "We are *so* engaged! I *slept* with you!"

"Shh," he said nervously, "your parents will hear you." He and Carolyn were sitting inside the gazebo in her backyard, hidden from view of the house, but Mitch knew all the windows in her house were open.

"I don't *care* if they hear me," she said through gritted teeth, but she had lowered her voice. "I don't care if the whole world hears me."

God, what was he going to do now? He had hoped she'd be reasonable. He had hoped that all he'd have to do was let her know he'd met someone else, and she wouldn't want to have anything more to do with him. Obviously that wasn't going to be the case.

"Carolyn," he said, "please...please calm down, okay? I didn't do this on purpose. I never meant to hurt you."

"You know, Mitchell Sinclair, you might think you're going to dump me, but you're not." She stood, planting her hands on her hips, and looked down at him. Her golden hair clung in damp ringlets against her small, heart-shaped face. Angry tears shimmered in her eyes.

Mitch felt like a heel. He knew her anger disguised a deeper pain. But what could he do? He wasn't going to marry her just because she expected it, or even because they'd had sex. He didn't love her. Actually, when she calmed down, she'd realize she was better off, too. She deserved to marry someone who would love her the way he loved Eve.

Firming his resolve, he stood, too. "I never meant for this to happen, but it did. I know you're angry and hurt, and I don't blame you, but I can't change things." He reached for her hand, but she yanked it away. "I hope one of these days you can forgive me," he said as he turned to leave the gazebo.

"Just where do you think you're going?" she snapped.

He stopped. "Carolyn..."

"You're not leaving."

He turned around slowly. "Please, let's not make this harder than it has to be."

Two brights spots of color had appeared on her cheeks. "I'm pregnant," she said. "Two months."

Mitch grabbed hold of the railing as her stark announcement thundered in his ears. "You...you can't be. "You're...I thought you were on the pill."

She smiled bitterly. "The pill isn't foolproof."

"But—" He broke off. Swallowed. Tried to think. "I—I don't—"

"Don't what?" she said, her eyes narrowing again. There was no hint of tears remaining. "Don't believe me? Don't believe this baby is yours?" Her voice rose with each word.

"Carolyn, please lower your voice," he said. His mind spun. Good Lord. Pregnant. "Can...can we sit down and talk about this?"

She plopped back down onto the seat, but her body was stiff and unyielding as he sat next to her and took her small hand in his. Her hand felt clammy and cold even though the July afternoon was sweltering and the air was thick with the promise of a summer storm.

Her eyes, flat and hostile, met his. "There's really nothing to talk about, is there? I'm pregnant, and you're the father."

"I...but we need to think about what we're going to do." Questions swirled in his brain. How could this have happened? Why had it happened? And especially now, when he'd met and fallen in love with Eve?

Oh, God. Eve.

What was he going to tell her?

"Do?" Carolyn laughed, the sound brittle and ugly. "I'll tell you exactly what we're going to do. I'm going to have this baby, and you're going to accept your responsibility as the father. We're going to get married—and very soon. That's what we're going to do.''

Mitch opened his mouth to protest.

''And if you think, for one minute, that things are going to be any other way, you've got another think coming. Because I'll tell my parents *and yours* exactly how you took advantage of me when I was feeling so low after Cliff died. And I think you know how they'll feel about *that!*''

Mitch closed his mouth and stared at her. He felt as if he were looking at a stranger. Where was the fragile, soft Carolyn who had wept for her lost love in his arms?

In that moment, Mitch knew he was trapped, just as surely and just as effectively as if he had a noose around his neck.

Eve's face—her sweet smile and her trusting eyes and her loving expression—floated through his mind. He remembered how he'd assured her everything would be all right.

He swallowed.

Nothing would ever be all right again.

Eve couldn't wait for her class reunion to be over. Her head pounded.

Why had she thought it would give her so much satisfaction to come back to Maple Hills? So far, all her return had given her was an upset stomach, jittery nerves and several headaches. Not to mention turbulent emotions and a reminder of everything that had hurt her so deeply all those years ago. She was a fool not to have realized that her past could never be safely tucked away like an old prom program.

Ever since she'd danced with Mitch last night, she hadn't been able to stop thinking about what he'd said. Why hadn't she questioned him about it? Why hadn't she danced with him again? She knew he would have asked her if she'd given him any encouragement at all.

Oh, she was so stupid! Why had it seemed so important to act as if she cared nothing for him? Now she'd be forever in the dark about why he and Carolyn had a fifteen-year-old son instead of a nineteen-year-old son.

She excused herself from the people with whom she'd been chatting and escaped to the ladies' room. God, she'd give anything to be able to leave. She freshened her makeup, noticing that there were faint circles under her eyes. While she stood there studying herself in the mirror, several women entered, their animated conversation fading as they realized she was there.

She smiled at them, recognizing none of them, then left. She searched the crowd for Jamie, finally spotting her on the other side of the room.

"Eve, you look tired," Jamie said when Eve reached her side.

"Does it show that much?"

Jamie nodded. "I'm tired myself. I had a really busy day, plus I think I'm coming down with a cold." She squeezed Eve's shoulder. "Why don't I tell Bob we're ready to leave?"

Eve smiled gratefully. She hadn't wanted to spoil Jamie's evening by cutting it short early, and several times she'd kicked herself for accepting the Zimmermans' offer of a ride tonight. She knew she could call a cab to take her back to the inn, but she also knew Jamie and Bob wouldn't let her do that. They'd insist on leaving with her.

On the way home, Eve once more felt grateful for Jamie's considerate silence. When Bob pulled under the covered entrance of the inn, Jamie got out of the car to give Eve a hug good-night.

"I hope this isn't goodbye," she said.

"No, of course not," Eve assured her. "We'll see each other again before I leave."

"When *are* you leaving?"

"I don't know. Originally, I'd planned to go back to New York on Monday, but I accepted a dinner invitation at the mayor's house for Monday night, so now I'm not sure. Maybe Tuesday."

"Gee, I'd love to have you come to our house, too. I want you to meet the kids. What are you doing tomorrow?"

Eve thought about the luncheon at Mitch's mother's house. After tonight, she was really dreading it. She simply didn't feel like exchanging niceties with the woman who had come so close to being her mother-in-law and the grandmother of her children. "I'm busy during the day, but I'm free tomorrow night."

"Good. Bob'll pick you up at six."

Later, after downing a couple of aspirin and taking a hot bath, which Eve hoped would relax her, she turned out the lights and tried to go to sleep.

Hours later, she knew it was hopeless.

She might never sleep again until she had completely relived and rehashed every single painful moment in her past.

Especially the most painful night of all.

Late July, twenty years earlier

All day Saturday Eve watched the clock. She and Mitch had arranged to meet at eight.

The hands of the kitchen clock seemed to creep around, slower and slower. And it was such a hot day, too, which somehow made the waiting even worse. If she hadn't had so much to look forward to, she would have gone crazy.

As it was, her stomach felt as if hundreds of butterflies were cavorting inside.

"Eve!"

Eve jumped and almost dropped the ceramic angel she'd been dusting.

Her mother stood in the doorway to the living room. "What's wrong with you today? I've called you twice and you didn't answer."

"I'm sorry, Mama. I—I guess I was daydreaming."

"I need for you to run over to Capellino's Market and get me some fresh oregano and a pound of butter."

Eve was grateful to escape. Anything to make the time go faster. By the time she returned from the market, it was almost five. She helped her mother put the finishing touches on their supper, which Eve's father always wanted promptly at six. They ate—Eve forcing herself to get some food down even though her stomach was so jumpy she was afraid she might throw up— then Eve helped Angela clean up and do the dishes. Finally it was seven-thirty, and Eve could escape.

"I'm going out now," she said, poking her head into the living room where her mother sat crocheting and her father sat watching TV.

Both parents looked up. Her mother frowned. "You've been out three times already this week, Eve. Can't you stay home once in a while?"

"Oh, Mama, everyone goes out on Saturday night. Besides, it's summer."

"So, since when do you have to do what everyone else does?" Angela replied. "If everyone jumps off a bridge, are you going to jump off a bridge, too?"

Eve sighed dramatically. "Mama..."

"Now, Angela," her father said mildly. "Eve is young. The young people, they like to be together. And soon enough she'll be in school again and she'll have to study at night. Let her have her fun now." He smiled at Eve.

Eve walked over and gave her father a grateful hug. "Thanks, Papa."

"You enjoy yourself, my angel."

"Hmm," was all her mother said. She peered at Eve over the tops of her half glasses, which she had to wear for close work. "Where are you going, and what time will you be home?"

"I don't know what we're going to do," Eve said, "but I'll be home by midnight, don't worry." She walked over to her mother, hugging and kissing her, too. "Bye!"

"Now remember what I've always told you," Angela said.

"I know, I know."

As Eve sped down the stairs, she thought that maybe tomorrow, once the future between her and Mitch was settled, she could have him come over to meet her parents. They would be surprised, maybe even angry for a while, but oh, in the end, they would forgive her for concealing her involvement with him, because they would love him, too, she just knew they would. How could they not? He was perfect. A delicious tingling excitement raced through her veins.

She was ready to explode by the time she reached the spot near the woods where Mitch always picked her up.

She hoped he wouldn't be late. She glanced at her watch. Almost eight. *Oh, Mitch, Mitch, hurry.*

A few seconds later, she saw him coming. Her heart gave a happy leap as he pulled his red convertible up to the curb and opened the door for her. She grinned as she hopped in. "Hi!" He looked so handsome in his tight jeans and dark green knit shirt, his hair ruffled because the top was down. She hadn't realized, until just this moment, how much she'd missed seeing him the past couple of days.

He smiled back. "Hi."

As was their custom, they did not kiss or touch. Even though this part of the road was fairly isolated, they had fallen into the habit of waiting until they were assured of privacy.

As Mitch pulled away from the curb and headed toward the other side of the lake, Eve waited for him to begin telling her what had happened when he'd confronted Carolyn.

He was silent, though, and his silence made Eve uneasy. Was something wrong? The thought made it hard for her to breathe. No. No. Of course not. Nothing was wrong. He was only waiting until he could park the car and give her his full attention. Of course. That was it. Silly for her to think anything was wrong. What could be wrong?

Maybe he changed his mind.

No! He wouldn't change his mind. He loved her. They loved each other. They were going to spend the rest of their lives together.

Why is he so quiet, then? Why doesn't he say something?

She was being stupid. What he had to say shouldn't be said casually. It was a serious subject. He must feel bad because Carolyn had probably been upset. His silence had nothing to do with *them*.

Despite her assurances to herself, as minute after minute passed in silence, Eve felt more and more anxious.

By the time they reached their place at the lake, she was half-sick with apprehension.

Mitch turned off the ignition, and in the sudden silence, the buzz of crickets and other insects filled the night. He didn't immediately turn toward her. His profile was a dark silhouette against the purple haze of twilight.

"Mitch?" Eve said. "What is it?"

He closed his eyes for one brief moment, then turned to look at her. The expression on his face was bleak.

Eve's heart lurched painfully.

"Eve... oh, Eve." He reached for her.

The kiss was desperate, filled with unspoken need and unhappiness.

He held her close afterward and whispered, "I'm sorry. I'm so sorry." Eve could feel his heart hammering in his chest. Fear clawed at her.

"Mitch, what's *wrong?*" she cried, pulling away so she could see his face. "You're scaring me!"

He swallowed. "Carolyn's pregnant. It's—it's my baby." His voice was ragged with misery. "And she's insisting that we get married next week."

It took a few seconds for the words to sink in. When they did, Eve couldn't breathe. She felt as if a great weight were pressing against her chest. She stared into Mitch's eyes, willing him to say he was only kidding. But she could see he wasn't.

"You... you mean, you *slept* with her, too?"

"I'm sorry," he whispered.

Her words were an anguished cry. "B-but how *could* you? You told me you didn't love her."

"I don't!" He put his head in his hands. "Oh, God, what a mess I've made of things."

Eve felt numb. She had known Mitch was experienced. Of course she had. But in her mind, his other partners had been vague, nameless girls in the distant past. No one important. No one who could hurt them. Finally she said, "Did you even tell her about us?"

He nodded wearily. "Yes. But it didn't make any difference to her. I even told her I didn't love her, but she doesn't care."

"But we...*we* love each other!" Tears clogged her throat. How could he marry someone else? He was going to marry *her!*

He leaned his forehead against hers. "Oh, Eve, I know, and you don't know how much I wish—" He broke off, taking a shaky breath. "I don't have any choice. I have to marry her."

Eve pushed him away. "No, you don't! You can't!"

"Eve, please, I—"

Eve buried her face in her hands. *No, no, no, no.*

"I don't blame you if you hate me," he said softly, stroking her hair. "I've really made a mess of things, haven't I?"

She couldn't answer. She still couldn't believe what he'd told her. Her heart was beating so fast it frightened her. She felt as if the entire world had crashed down upon her head, and that she would never see daylight again.

Eve slept late on Sunday morning after the reunion. The phone woke her at nine-thirty.

"Miss DelVecchio? This is Pamela Sinclair. I do hope it's not too early to be calling."

"No, of course not," Eve said, struggling to clear the cobwebs from her brain.

"I am so sorry, but I'm going to have to cancel the luncheon in your honor today," Pamela said, and now Eve heard the distress in the older woman's voice. She rushed on before Eve could answer. "I've done the stupidest thing! Oh, I'm *so* angry with myself! Imagine a woman of my age being so careless! It's really maddening."

God, Eve badly needed a cup of coffee.

"I had the most frustrating accident last night," Pamela continued without pause. "Clifford and I were playing in a bridge tournament in Columbus, and when we left the hotel, I tripped and fell down several steps."

"Oh, dear, I'm sorry," Eve said, coming fully awake now.

"And I've not only broken my ankle, I've torn several ligaments in my foot and leg, so now I've got this awful cast practically up to my knee, and the doctor *insists* that I stay off my feet for six weeks! Oh, it's so very frustrating, I just can't afford to lose six weeks, and I'm so sorry about—"

"Mrs. Sinclair, please don't give it another thought," Eve interrupted. "I'm a little under the weather myself, so you've actually done me a favor because now I can just rest here at the hotel this afternoon." She felt terrible about Pamela's accident, but she couldn't help also feeling relieved that she wouldn't have to face today's ordeal.

"But I did so want to meet you. . . ."

"I know. I was looking forward to meeting you, too. But now the important thing is taking care of that foot."

"Maybe we could do it another time," Pamela said hopefully.

"I'm sorry, but I'm planning to leave Maple Hills Tuesday morning. Maybe on my next visit..."

"Well..."

Eve could hear Mitch's mother's disappointment. She knew she could offer to stop by Pamela's house today, just to say hello, but as much as Eve had once thought she'd like to meet the woman who might have been her mother-in-law, she simply wasn't up to any more emotional turmoil right now. This cancellation was a gift, and Eve had no intention of doing anything stupid like rejecting it.

So she said goodbye pleasantly but firmly.

After thinking about the phone call for a few minutes, she called the front desk. It was a relief to find the weekend manager on duty, rather than the suffocatingly attentive Mr. French. "Can you recommend a good local florist?" she asked.

She hoped the lavish bouquet that would be delivered later that morning would make up for at least a portion of Pamela Sinclair's disappointment.

As Eve drank her room service coffee and prepared to face the day, she decided that the canceled luncheon was more than a gift. It was a sign.

A sign that it was time for her to pack up her marbles and go home.

Chapter Seven

"And this is Renee," Jamie said proudly.

An attractive youngster already evincing signs of her mother's height and lean grace walked forward. Jamie put her arm around her daughter.

Renee smiled shyly. "Hello, Miss DelVecchio."

Eve returned her smile and pretended the ache around her heart did not exist. "Hello, Renee. It's very nice to meet you. But please, I'd like you to call me Eve."

"Oh, I can't do *that*," Renee said. "My mom would kill me!"

Jamie chuckled. "Now, sweetie, you know I wouldn't kill you." She turned to Eve. "I insist that the children use proper forms of address when talking to adults. I hate it when kids call me Jamie like they're one of my contemporaries!"

It was Eve's turn to laugh softly. "I never would've

imagined I'd hear the original Maple Hills rebel spouting such conservative opinions.''

"Shh," Jamie said in mock horror. "My kids don't know about my past indiscretions."

"What indiscretions?" Bob called out from the kitchen, where he was busy making his famous Caesar salad, as Jamie had fondly told Eve earlier.

"Yeah, Mom," said Robert, the Zimmermans' fourteen-year-old son, who had just entered the family room. "What indiscretions?"

"See? Now you've gone and done it." Jamie grinned at Eve. "They won't let me rest until I tell all."

"Be sure and tell 'em how you burned your bra," Eve said sotto voce.

"Oh, we know about that, that's old stuff," Robert said, walking over and ruffling his mother's hair. "We want to know about the stuff she *didn't* tell us!"

"There's nothing else to tell. Actually, I was a perfect child. Never gave my parents a single gray hair," Jamie said, winking at Eve.

Rachel, who was setting the table, rolled her eyes. "We know. We know. You walked two miles to school in knee-high snow, right?"

Eve laughed aloud. "Is that what she told you?"

"You mean it's not true?" Bob said.

All the Zimmermans laughed. Jamie smiled happily.

Eve liked this family. This was the first time she'd really felt comfortable since coming back to Maple Hills. Still . . . their easy banter and obvious love for one another was a poignant reminder of everything she didn't have.

Would never have.

All through dinner, as their unity and devotion were reinforced by everything they said and did, Eve couldn't help comparing her life to Jamie's.

It was true that Eve had everything money could buy: furs, jewels, homes—including a spacious apartment overlooking Central Park, a restored Victorian home on Martha's Vineyard, and a snug A-frame cabin tucked in the mountains near Aspen—while Jamie had only this ordinary ranch house in a middle-class subdivision on the outskirts of Maple Hills and had casually admitted to Eve that money was always tight.

It was also true that Eve had reached heights few people ever reached, attaining great success in a highly competitive business and, in the process, become famous and rich. She routinely hobnobbed with royalty and movie stars. She was listed in *Who's Who in America*. Everywhere she went people catered to her and envied her.

Jamie was just a wife and mother in a small town.

Eve knew all this.

She knew how lucky she was.

She knew millions of women would eagerly change places with her.

And yet, each time one of the Zimmerman children called Jamie ''Mom,'' Eve ached inside.

She had missed so much. So very much.

What she wouldn't give to hear her child call her ''Mom''—just once. To have her child draw her forward and say proudly, ''This is my mother,'' to his friends.

What she wouldn't give for the right to whip out pictures, to boast of her child's accomplishments the way the Zimmermans boasted of theirs.

Eve tried not to think this way. Thinking this way was useless. The past was past. She had done what she thought was right. It couldn't be changed. There was no sense questioning decisions made years ago.

But tonight, sitting around the Zimmermans' table, for the first time in years, she wondered if she'd made a mistake.

Mid-August, twenty years earlier

For weeks after Mitch broke up with her, Eve walked around like a zombie.

Not eating.

Not sleeping.

Barely speaking.

She was filled with a pain so enormous she actually felt physically ill and half-nauseated most of the time. On the day the announcement of the marriage of Mitchell Emerson Sinclair and Carolyn Louise Whittaker appeared in the paper, Eve did throw up, several times.

Her parents were worried sick. They hovered over her. "What is wrong?" they asked again and again.

Eve only shook her head. "Nothing's wrong," she said dully.

Eve knew her parents were whispering about her, trying to figure out what to do about her, but she couldn't seem to rouse herself enough to care. She only knew she had lost Mitch, and nothing else seemed to matter. It was all she could do to just get through each day without breaking down.

It might have helped if she'd had someone to talk to, but Jamie was still in Florida, and there was no one else Eve trusted enough.

So she dragged through the days and tried not to think of the future.

And then one morning, when she was kneeling on the bathroom floor rooting around the bottom shelf of the bathroom cupboard for the rubbing alcohol, her attention was caught by something shoved back into the corner.

A small pink box.

Her tampons.

She stared at it, frowning.

Suddenly she scrambled to her feet and dashed into her bedroom, slamming the door behind her. Her heart pumped frantically. Her gaze darted to the calendar on her bedroom wall. She yanked it off its hook, turned the current page back so the month of July was exposed, and stared at the lack of any notation.

She flipped the page to June. Stared. Nothing.

She swallowed, closing her eyes. A silent prayer shuddered through her body. *Hail, Mary, full of grace, the Lord is with thee. Blessed art thou amongst women . . .*

Biting her lower lip, trying to keep from going to pieces, she sank down on the side of her bed and slowly turned the page back to May.

And there, in red ink, just like she'd kept track of her menstrual period for the past five years, was the little notation in the square for May eleventh.

Her initials: E.D.

The knowledge crashed through her.

May eleventh!

Today was August nineteenth.

She had not had a period for more than three months.

How could this be? How could she not have realized this before now? *Oh, God, oh, God.* She hadn't noticed because she'd been in another world—so wrapped up in Mitch, so completely nutty over him, that being with him, seeing him, was all she'd thought about since that first night.

Her hands shook as she dropped the calendar.

It couldn't be! Every time, Mitch had carefully used a condom, because Eve wasn't on the pill like so many girls her age. His consideration and protection of her had been one of the things she most loved about him.

All except that first time.

Because that first time, their lovemaking hadn't been planned. *Please, God, it was only that one time! You wouldn't do this to me, would you?*

But her denial didn't change the facts. She had not had a period since early May. And even though she was irregular, she had never gone more than thirty-five days between periods.

The knowledge sank into her like a heavy stone sinking into a shallow pond.

She must be pregnant. There was no other explanation.

She held her stomach and rocked back and forth. What was she going to do? If she'd felt desperate before, when she knew she'd lost Mitch, she felt completely panic-stricken now.

Her parents would die when they found out. They were so old-fashioned. So straitlaced. They expected so much of her.

She was ruined!

How could she ever tell them?

And if she could somehow find the courage, then what? She thought of her mother. How proud she was of Eve's accomplishments. How often she had warned Eve about the perils of sex outside of marriage. She thought of her father. His old-world morals and his strict ideas of right and wrong. He would demand to know who the father was. He would insist that Mitch take responsibility for her and her child.

She would die before she'd ask Mitch for anything. If he didn't want her, she didn't want anything from him. Besides, he was already married to Carolyn. So there was no counting on Mitch for anything. No, she would have to figure this problem out for herself.

Her mind raced.

What should she do? What *could* she do? Go away somewhere? Have the baby and try to raise it alone? But how? She had no skills. She'd never even held a job except for baby-sitting. Her father had never wanted her to work while she was in school.

School!

She bit her lip. She was supposed to start college in less than two weeks. Oh, God. She couldn't start college now. How could she let her parents pay for the semester when she would not be able to continue with her studies past January?

What was she going to do?

She thought about staying here in Maple Hills. Having the baby. Having everyone whisper about her. Seeing the knowing looks. Hearing the snickers from her school friends. And what if someone figured out that Mitch was the father? Eve had no way of knowing for sure that she hadn't been seen with him by someone who knew her. Wouldn't the town gossips have a field day with that piece of knowledge?

She'd rather die!

Around and around her mind whirled.

She would have to leave. But how?

She knew she was going to need help, and her mind automatically turned to the one person who had always been there for her—her brother, Tony.

She immediately felt calmer. Tony. Of course. Tony would know what to do. Tony always knew what to do to make things right.

Suddenly filled with purpose, she went into the bathroom, washed her face and brushed her teeth, then carefully applied makeup until all traces of her tears were gone. She would have to use a pay phone to call her brother. Her only problem would be getting out of the house without her parents knowing.

She was in luck. Her mother had gone down into the shop—probably to help Eve's father—and Eve sneaked out without either of them hearing or seeing her.

She crossed her fingers as she dialed Anthony's number. *Please be there.* Her luck held. He answered on the second ring.

"Oh, Tony, thank God you're home. I have to talk to you. And I don't want Mama and Papa to know. Can...can you invite me to visit and make it sound like it's your idea?"

He never questioned her, and she blessed him for it. He didn't even hesitate, just said, "When do you want to come?"

The following day she flew to Connecticut.

When she arrived, she tearfully told Tony and Mary Ann the whole story. The only part she left out was Mitch's name. She knew Tony's reaction would be identical to her father's. He would want to confront Mitch and demand he do the right thing by her.

"I don't understand why you won't tell me who the father is," Tony said.

"Because h-he's married," Eve said.

"Eve!" Mary Ann said, her face mirroring her shock. Tony shook his head disbelievingly.

Eve realized they both thought she meant she'd been seeing a married man. She started to correct them, then thought it might actually be better for them to think this, because that way they would stop badgering her. But inwardly she cringed. Now she must appear even lower in their eyes than she had before.

"So what do you want to do?" Tony asked. "Do you want to keep the baby?"

Eve swallowed. "I—I don't see how I can. I—I thought maybe you'd help me find an agency where I c-could place the baby for adoption." It hurt even to say the words. Whenever Eve had dreamed about having a baby, she had imagined being wildly happy, with a smiling father standing beside her. Never had she believed something like this would happen to her.

Tony and Mary Ann exchanged a glance. "Eve," Tony said slowly, "you know how Mary Ann and I have always wanted a baby?"

Well, yes, Eve had known. "Are you saying you... you might want to adopt my baby?"

Mary Ann nodded eagerly, and Tony said, "It's the best way. Everything'll be in the family, and no one else will ever have to know." He smiled in satisfaction. "It's perfect."

And so was born the fiction of the out-of-the-blue call from the adoption agency who had finally found a child for Tony and Mary Ann to adopt.

Eve was grateful. So grateful, she had happily agreed to keep the identity of her baby a secret from everyone.

"That's our only condition," Tony had stressed. "Because anything else wouldn't be fair to us." He pursed his lips. "Course, Mama and Papa will have to

know, because there's no way they'll buy you staying
here otherwise.''

Eve swallowed. But she agreed to everything. After
all, what choice did she have?

Mitch spent Sunday night thinking about all the
might-have-beens in his life. What might have been if
Cliff hadn't died. What might have been if Mitch himself hadn't succumbed to the seductive pull of Carolyn's grief and need. What might have been if only he'd
had the guts to stand up to Carolyn and to face the
wrath of his family. To fight for what he wanted and to
insist that Carolyn see a doctor with Mitch right there
beside her when she did.

What might have been if Carolyn hadn't lied.

Mitch would never forget the day he'd found out she
wasn't really pregnant.

She'd tried to make him believe that she'd really
thought she was. She'd sworn that she hadn't lied to
him. But he could see the lie in her eyes. He could feel
it in the nauseated roll of his stomach. He knew it in his
heart.

For days after he'd discovered the lie, he had walked
around in a numb sort of lethargy. He had gone to
classes, come home to the apartment in New Haven that
he now shared with his wife of six weeks, even made an
effort to pretend everything was normal.

But his heart was empty, and his emotions were dead.
He couldn't even drum up a healthy dose of anger, because he could see the fear Carolyn was trying to suppress. He knew she was scared he would leave her.

He almost did.

He would have, if there'd been any hope of getting
Eve back. Despite the fact that his parents would be

furious with him, that they might even withdraw their financial support, he would have given up everything. But then he realized he'd lost Eve for good.

After the numbness wore off, he had called Eve's home—only the second or third time he'd ever done so. Her mother answered. When Mitch asked for Eve, her mother said she wasn't living there any longer.

Mitch just assumed Eve was at school. He said he was an old high school friend and he wanted to get in touch with her. He asked for her number at O.S.U.

"She didn't go to O.S.U.," her mother said. "She's at her brother's in Connecticut."

Mitch frowned. At her brother's in Connecticut? But why? Was she going to school there? "Could I, uh, have the number there?" he asked, half-afraid she would refuse. Eve had told him how old-fashioned her mother was. Maybe she would be suspicious. Maybe she would ask his name. Maybe Eve had told her parents about him.

But Eve's mother gave him the number without asking any questions.

Mitch's fingers trembled as he dialed.

A woman answered. It wasn't Eve.

"Hello," he said. "May I speak to Eve DelVecchio, please?"

"Uh, Eve isn't here right now," the woman said. "Would you like to leave a message?"

Mitch was calling from a pay phone. He had no number to leave. "No, I—I can't. I won't be at this number much longer. What time do you expect her back? I'll call her back."

"Well, I don't know," the woman said doubtfully. "Probably late . . . around midnight."

Midnight. He couldn't call her at midnight. "What about tomorrow? What time will she be home tomorrow? I'll call her then."

"I really have no idea. It's best if you just leave your name and number. She's very hard to catch at home."

Mitch hung up.

The following day he left his apartment before eight, walked to the closest pay phone, and called again. He'd decided early in the morning was the best time to try to reach Eve.

This time a male voice answered.

When Mitch asked for Eve, the man said, "She's not here. Who is this?"

"J-just a friend." Mitch could have kicked himself for stammering, but the man's tone—Mitch assumed it was her brother speaking—was intimidating. Almost belligerent.

There was silence for a long moment. Then her brother said in a low, tight voice, "I know who you are, you're the scum bag who's married and who has no right to be calling my sister. I've got just one thing to say to a lowlife like you. Stay away from her, 'cause if you don't, I'll make you sorry you were ever born!"

Then the phone went dead in Mitch's ear.

The next day, he and Carolyn told their parents she'd miscarried, because Mitch saw no point in upsetting them by telling them the truth. Especially now that he'd decided the best option left to him was to try to make a success of his marriage.

Chapter Eight

Mitch wondered if he should have refused the dinner invitation from Ann Marie and Terry Flynn. What was the point to seeing Eve again? Seeing her only made him realize how much he had given up when he'd let her go. Seeing her only filled him with regret for the past and kindled the dissatisfaction he already felt for the present and the future.

Well, it was too late to back out now, he thought as he pulled up in front of the Flynns' graceful two-story Colonial. Only one other car was parked outside—a gray Mercedes—and if Mitch wasn't mistaken it belonged to Ann Marie's sister Alana and her husband Pete. Good. The evening would be easier to get through with the buffer of another couple besides Terry and Ann Marie.

Mitch fought down the nervousness that threatened to overtake him as he rang the front doorbell. *Come on, you can get through one more evening, no sweat.* Hell, if he'd lived through all those years with Carolyn, pretending to the entire world that they had a perfect marriage, he could get through one night with an old flame.

Terry opened the door, a big grin lighting his face. "Hey, Mitch," he said. "Come on in. Say, I heard about your mother. How's she doing?"

"Complaining."

Terry laughed. "Can't say as I blame her. I hate being laid up. Ann Marie says I'm an awful patient."

Mitch handed his host the two bottles of Johannesburg Riesling he'd carefully selected.

"Thanks," Terry said. "Ann Marie's putting the finishing touches on dinner. I'll just take these out to the kitchen, but the others are in the living room. Go on in. Oh, and help yourself to a drink from the bar. You know where everything is."

When Mitch entered the elegantly furnished room, the first person he saw was Eve. She stood with her back to him, talking to Alana and Pete. His heart gave a little hop of awareness. He told himself once again to settle down.

In the moments before the others spotted him, he quietly studied her.

She looked sensational, every inch the New York sophisticate. Her slender figure was shown to advantage in a short black cocktail dress of simple lines. She wore dark stockings with her black sparkly pumps, and a thick diamond bracelet glittered from her right wrist. Her dark hair was pinned up tonight, exposing her long, graceful neck, and when she turned slightly, he saw that large diamond studs adorned her earlobes.

Mitch was suddenly glad he'd worn his nicest gray suit paired with an expensive designer shirt that had been one of last year's Christmas gifts from his parents.

Alana noticed him and smiled and gave a little wiggly wave with her fingers.

Eve turned, her gaze connecting with his, and he got his second jolt of the evening. How did she manage to make him feel as inexperienced and unsure of himself as a green lawyer trying his first case?

Determined not to show how she affected him, he smiled and walked forward. "Hi," he said, including all three in his greeting.

"Hi, Mitch," said Alana. "You're looking *good* tonight." She sipped from her glass of wine and studied him over the rim, hazel eyes sparkling.

His smile expanded. "You are, too. Green's your color."

"Thank you, kind sir."

He casually turned to Eve. "You also look terrific tonight."

"Thank you." She seemed perfectly calm. Perfectly composed. And perfectly unaffected by his presence as she, too, sipped from a glass of wine.

Mitch and Pete shook hands. "Missed you the other night," Mitch said, remembering that Pete hadn't accompanied Alana to the reception given in Eve's honor.

"Alana told me it was a great bash," Pete said.

"Speaking of great bashes," Alana said, "Eve was just telling us about her class reunion."

"Did you enjoy it?" Mitch asked.

Eve's eyes met his again. Every time he looked down into their soft blue-gray depths, he felt at a disadvantage, yet he couldn't seem to tear his gaze away.

She shrugged, smiling slightly. "You know how it is when you spend an evening with people you don't know well. After the first catching up, you struggle to find something to talk about.''

He nodded, but he didn't really know how it was, because he'd spent his entire life, except for college and law school, right here in Maple Hills, surrounded by people he'd known forever.

''What she's too polite to say,'' Alana remarked dryly, ''is that she lives in a different world than we do here in Maple Hills.''

''No, that's not it,'' Eve quickly objected. ''I didn't mean what I said to sound as if I was bored or anything. I feel the same way in New York when I go to a large function where I don't know a lot of the other guests. I don't like making idle chitchat, and I don't enjoy gossip. I guess I'm really kind of a private person. I most enjoy quiet evenings alone or with a good friend or two. Big gatherings have never been my forte, and unfortunately—'' she grimaced ''—in my business, I can't avoid them.''

It was hard for Mitch to believe that she would ever be uncomfortable in any situation. She seemed perfectly poised and self-assured. But her words had the ring of sincerity, and for the first time since her return, he wondered if maybe her life wasn't as perfect as he'd imagined it to be. Maybe there were drawbacks to being as successful as she was. Well, of course, there were. He had always known that. He'd just forgotten it in the wake of insecurity that had come from seeing her again and reincarnating all of his past mistakes.

''I never would have guessed you weren't perfectly at home during the reception Friday night,'' Alana said. ''You impressed everyone with how easy you were to talk to and how much you seemed to be enjoying yourself.''

Eve smiled. "Good. I'd hate for any one of those nice people to think I wasn't flattered to be there."

For a few seconds, no one said anything. Mitch excused himself and walked over to the bar. He decided he'd rather have a Scotch and water instead of wine, so he fixed his drink, then carried it back to the group.

Just then, Terry and Ann Marie entered the living room. Mitch kissed Ann Marie's cheek, complimented her appearance, and after a few moments of more talk, Ann Marie announced that dinner was ready.

Pete offered Alana his arm.

Mitch looked at Eve. "May I?" he said. He held out his right arm.

She took it, looking up briefly before they followed Alana and Pete into the dining room. And in that crystal moment when their gazes clung, Mitch knew he still wanted her.

Eve's emotions once again felt raw and exposed. Making things worse, she was seated across the table from Mitch instead of next to him, so she couldn't avoid looking at him. It seemed as if every few minutes, their gazes would connect, and her stomach would clench.

Why did he affect her this way?

What was her problem?

You're still attracted to him. That's the problem. You knew it the other night. Why are you pretending you're not?

Yes, it was true. Mitch still had the power to turn her knees to jelly. It frustrated her that this could be so. Hadn't she learned her lesson? Hadn't she suffered enough at the hands of this man? Why couldn't she relegate him to the trash heap where he belonged? Why did he continue to have this power over her?

He affects you this way because he's the father of your child. Because you've never been able to forget about him. Because every time you look at Matthew, you see Mitch. That's why. The two of you have unfinished business.

Alana broke into Eve's thoughts by saying, "I know you said you don't like gossip, Eve, but I'm dying to hear about all the famous people you know. Have you met Calvin Klein?"

Eve gratefully turned her attention Alana's way. "Yes, I know him. The fashion industry is like any other—actually like a world of its own—and most people involved in it know everyone."

"How about models? Do you know Cindy Crawford?" Pete asked.

Alana rolled her eyes.

Eve laughed. "I've met her," she admitted.

"Is she as beautiful in person as she is in the ads?" Pete asked.

"Please say she isn't," Alana said.

"Unfortunately, I'm afraid she is," Eve said.

Alana wrinkled her nose. "I was afraid of that."

They all laughed, and from then on the conversation was lively, with everyone asking Eve about other fashion world figures. Mitch didn't join in the questioning, though. He just sat and listened and watched her, and Eve wondered what he was thinking. Normally she wouldn't have wanted to talk about the famous people she knew or had met. She considered that kind of talk bragging, especially with people like these, but tonight—probably because her feelings unnerved her—she needed for Mitch to see how far she'd come from that long-ago girl from the other side of the tracks who had hung on his every word and felt so honored by his attention.

The shoe is on the other foot now, she thought. *I'm the important one here—not you—and I don't intend to let you forget it.*

When dinner was over, they lingered over coffee and dessert—a mouth-watering rhubarb pie that Eve knew she shouldn't be eating, but she ate, anyway—and the talk turned to a recent case of Mitch's.

"I never thought you had a prayer of winning that case," Terry said.

"Yeah, impressed the hell out of me," added Pete.

"Mitch represented a young woman who was suing the law firm she had worked for for wrongful dismissal," Ann Marie explained. "And the law firm just happens to be one of the largest and most influential in the state."

Eve had been avoiding looking directly at Mitch for a while, but politeness deemed that now she must. "Sounds interesting," she said.

"It was a challenge," he said. "Because wrongful dismissal is difficult to prove, especially when the employees who might have corroborated my client's story weren't inclined to testify."

"Afraid they'd get fired, too," Pete said.

"It certainly happens," Terry said.

"I was lucky, though," Mitch said, "because my client had kept a notebook, with dates, and at the eleventh hour, I was able to persuade a key witness to back up her story."

"It was really a big deal here in Maple Hills," Ann Marie said, "because the young woman is the daughter of a very well liked and respected teacher at the high school. We were all pulling for her."

Mitch smiled. "It could've gone either way. There's no telling with juries."

"You're so modest, Mitch," Ann Marie said.

"Not modest, just realistic."

"He's modest," Ann Marie said, looking at Eve.

The conversation intrigued Eve, because it showed her another side of Mitch. Funny, but she hadn't thought about him in terms of what he'd been doing professionally all these years. She had never once wondered if he was a successful lawyer or what kind of law he practiced or whether he was well-thought-of.

Obviously he was. His friends certainly seemed to have a lot of respect for him. And his friends were educated, intelligent people that Eve had come to admire in the short time she'd known them.

The conversation turned to a controversial zoning ordinance that was up for consideration before the city council that week, and Eve sat back and mostly listened, even though the talk wasn't boring. In fact, when Pete and Mitch got into a spirited debate, with Pete for the zoning and Mitch very much against it, she found herself cheering for Mitch.

"The thing is, Pete," he said, finishing his argument, "if that ordinance passes, it will only benefit the well-off of Maple Hills."

"Of which you're one," Pete said.

"Exactly. Which means I have an obligation to look out for those who aren't as lucky as I am and who haven't the resources to fight for themselves."

Eve didn't want to admire Mitch. She didn't want to admit that he had become the kind of man she would have been proud to be with. She wanted to hate him. She wanted him to be a sleaze so she could tell herself she was better off without him.

About ten o'clock, Ann Marie yawned. "Oh, gosh, I'm sorry," she said. "It's not the company, believe me!"

Alana scooted her chair back. "I'm tired, too, and I've gotta get up early." She picked up her dessert plate and coffee cup.

"No, no," Ann Marie said, "leave everything. Terry and I'll do that after you're gone."

Everyone rose. Thank-yous and good-nights were said. Hands were shaken. Cheeks were kissed.

Eve turned to Terry. "Would you mind calling a cab for me?" she asked quietly.

"Oh, that's not necessary. I'm sure Pete or Mitch would be glad to drive you back to the hotel," Terry said.

"No, I don't want to trouble—"

"I heard that, and it's no trouble at all," Mitch said, walking up to them. He smiled down at her. "Are you ready to leave now?"

Eve couldn't think of a graceful way to refuse his offer. And even if she could, she wasn't sure she wanted to. Right now, she wasn't sure of anything. "Whenever you're ready," she said. She hoped her eyes didn't give away her inner turmoil.

A few minutes later, they walked out into the balmy summer night. A full moon illuminated the front lawn, bathing it in silvery light. The fragrance of climbing roses perfumed the air. Somewhere down the street, a dog barked. It was a scene of perfect tranquility, yet Eve felt anything but tranquil. Mitch's hand at her elbow, his solid male presence at her side, the clean, fresh scent of his cologne—all conspired to keep her off balance and edgy.

When they reached his car, he unlocked the passenger side and helped her in. They didn't speak. Her heart was beating too fast, and she told herself to calm down.

Don't be an idiot. It's just a ride home.

When he got in and started the ignition, she tried not to think about all the other times they'd spent in a car of his. Of course, this plush import was nothing like that old red Mustang convertible, and they were nothing like those kids had been, either.

She especially was no longer naive.

She no longer believed in happy endings and Prince Charmings and white horses.

"Nice party, wasn't it?" he said as he pulled away from the curb and headed down the quiet tree-lined street.

"Yes." Then, because she felt she had to say something else or maybe give him the idea she was uncomfortable, she added, "They're all very nice people."

"Yes, they are." He reached down, pushed a cassette into the cassette drive. In moments, Bonnie Raitt's voice singing "Let's Give Them Something to Talk About" filled the air.

Eve smiled inwardly. Oh, yes. How appropriate. She could give this whole town something really juicy to talk about if she wanted to.

Amused by her thoughts, she slid a sideways glance at Mitch. Unexpectedly her throat tightened as she stared at his profile. Her flip thoughts slid away as she stared at him—at the strong jawline and the high bridge of his nose—at the way his lips curved and his hair grew. This was how Matthew would look when he was Mitch's age.

Shaken, she turned away.

They were silent the rest of the way to the inn. Eve was thankful the ride wasn't a long one.

She had expected Mitch to pull into the curving driveway at the entrance to the hotel, but instead he turned toward the side lot.

"You can just drop me in front," she said.

He ignored her, driving into the lot and pulling into a vacant parking slot. He switched off the ignition before answering. "I'd hoped maybe we could walk in the garden for a while. I wanted a chance to talk privately."

What could she say? *No, thanks, Mitch. I'd rather not.* Well, she could, of course. But wouldn't he think she was afraid to talk to him if she did? "All right," she said.

The Maple Hills Inn was famous throughout the region for its English-inspired gardens. Eve took Mitch's arm as they headed down the main path.

He stopped when they reached the center fountain, which was circled by several wooden benches. After making sure the one he'd selected was dry, he offered her a seat. Then he sat next to her—not too close, though—and casually draped his arm across the back of the bench.

Eve took a deep breath. She hoped she was up to this.

"Eve..." His voice was soft.

She slowly looked around, raising her eyes to meet his.

"The other night...I know there was something you wanted to ask."

She wanted to look away, but she couldn't.

"I know you were wondering why my son is only fifteen, why I didn't mention a child nineteen or so, and I feel I owe you an explanation."

"You don't owe me anything."

"I do, and we both know it." He sighed heavily. "Carolyn wasn't pregnant when I married her. She'd lied to me."

Eve wasn't sure why she believed him, but she did. She nodded slowly. "When did you find out?"

"When she supposedly had a miscarriage but didn't want to see a doctor," he said bitterly.

Eve looked down at her hands, which were folded in her lap. "Thank you for telling me, but that's all in the past. It's not really important anymore."

"It's important to me."

He reached around, tipping her chin up so that she was forced to look at him again. "I hated her when I found out. I hated her because I'd lost you."

Eve's heart began to beat faster. *Oh, Mitch.*

"I called you, you know."

Eve blinked. "When?"

"When I found out she'd lied."

"Where did you call me? At home?"

"Yes, and then I called at your brother's because your mother told me that's where you were living."

Eve could see he was telling her the truth. She bit her lip in consternation. Why hadn't Tony told her about the call? "I never knew you'd called," she finally said.

Mitch grimaced. "I'm not surprised. Your brother was really mad. He called me a scum bag and a lowlife and told me not to try to see you because if I did, he'd make me sorry I was ever born."

Eve swallowed. Tony had only been trying to protect her. Hadn't he? "I'm sorry."

"Hey, I had it coming. In his shoes, I'd have probably done the same thing."

She nodded.

"After that, even though I'd decided to stay with Carolyn, for months all I thought about was you...and about how stupid I'd been. It was a long time before I could forgive her...and an even longer time before I could forgive myself."

They stared at each other. All kinds of emotions tumbled through Eve's mind. And then, slowly, he lowered his head.

Eve knew she should pull back.

She knew this was a mistake.

Even as she told herself this, she lifted her lips to meet his.

Chapter Nine

The kiss began as just a light brush of lips against lips. Then Mitch settled his mouth more firmly against hers, nudging it open with his tongue and tasting her fully. She shuddered, and immediately all his senses leaped to life as desire jackknifed through him. His last coherent thought before he was completely lost in a whirlpool of sensations was how completely right she felt in his arms.

He kissed her deeply and hungrily, his hands roaming over her back in eager exploration. She kissed him in return, and it was as if all the years that had passed had never been. He felt just as excited, just as filled with awe and wonder as he'd felt all those years ago.

It wasn't until the sound of a car door slamming shut, accompanied by animated voices, penetrated Mitch's brain that he remembered they were sitting in a public garden where anyone could walk by and see them.

Reluctantly he broke the kiss, but he continued to hold her close. He cupped her face, keeping it tipped so that he could look down into her eyes. "I've dreamed of holding you like this for a long time," he whispered.

"I...this isn't a good idea, Mitch." Her voice sounded breathless as she tried to pull away.

His arms tightened around her possessively. "Why not?" Forgetting about the possibility of spectators, he tried to kiss her again, but she turned her head and his lips skimmed her cheek instead.

"Please, Mitch, stop..." she said weakly as he trailed his mouth to her ear, then down to her neck. She trembled, and an involuntary moan escaped her lips as he touched his tongue to a hollow in her throat. Her pulse fluttered wildly.

"Do you really want me to stop?" His hand crept around to gently cup her breast.

She gasped as his thumb grazed the nipple.

"Don't." She pushed his hand away. "Please don't."

Mitch sighed and released her. "Don't worry. I'm not going to force you." He willed his own heart to slow down. "No matter what you say, Eve, I don't think anything has changed between us. I think you still want me just as much as I want you."

She lowered her head. The back of her neck seemed particularly sweet and vulnerable to Mitch. He was filled with an aching tenderness that was nearly as strong as the desire that still raged through his body. His hands itched to touch her. His mouth yearned to kiss her. But he forced himself to sit quietly. He would not try to coerce her. If she came to him, he wanted her to come of her own free will.

Nothing less would satisfy him.

After a few seconds, she said, "There's no point to this, you know. We can't go back. The past is the past."

"I don't want us to go back. I want us to go forward."

She shook her head. "It's not that simple."

"Why isn't it?" He wanted her to look at him. He touched her chin.

She sighed. "We're different people than we were twenty years ago, Mitch. A lot has happened. Things have changed."

"This hasn't changed." And even though he'd told himself he wouldn't coerce her, his grip on her chin tightened, and he lowered his head and captured her mouth again. This time the kiss was hard and demanding, and after a few seconds of stiff resistance, she wound her arms around his neck and returned the kiss with a greedy passion that made his heart soar with triumph.

When they broke apart, they were both breathing fast. "See?" he said raggedly. "You can't deny that there are still strong feelings between us."

Her eyes gleamed in the moonlight. "I won't deny there's still a physical attraction, but I've been physically attracted to many men without acting upon that attraction. Especially when I knew the man in question wasn't someone I wanted in my life."

Mitch didn't believe she really meant what she'd said. He wanted to take her into his arms. He wanted to kiss her senseless and erase every single one of her objections. He especially wanted to make love to her. He wanted to show her how much she still meant to him, how much she'd always meant to him. He particularly wanted to show her how sorry he was for all the lost years.

But he knew he'd better not. The moment was fragile. The wrong word, the wrong action, could scare her away. Permanently.

He couldn't take that chance.

She was here, finally, and he wanted to keep her here—at least long enough to find out if the torrent of emotions unleashed between them tonight was real.

He forced himself to speak quietly and calmly. "I wish you weren't leaving tomorrow. I wish we had more time to talk. To get to know each other again. Maybe then you wouldn't feel this way."

She nodded slowly. "Yes, I—I do, too." The cascading water of the fountain behind her provided a sparkling backwash of light that framed her slender figure and haloed her hair.

"Do you *have* to leave tomorrow?"

"I... no, I guess not, but—"

"Then don't."

"Mitch..." She looked away, staring off toward the hotel.

He could see that she was biting her bottom lip, and he smiled, remembering it was a nervous habit she'd had even when she was young. "Please, Eve. Stay at least a few more days."

"I don't know..."

Hope flamed. She was wavering. Pressing his advantage, he said urgently, "Please, Eve. Stay at least one more day and be my guest for dinner tomorrow night."

She sighed again. "All right. I'll stay."

Relief made Mitch feel weak. He wasn't out of the woods yet, but at least now he felt he had a fighting chance.

* * *

There were times when Eve simply had to hear Matthew's voice. Tonight was one of them.

The moment she unlocked the door to her suite, she headed straight for the phone. Although it was after eleven, she knew Matthew would not be asleep. She also knew late at night was the best time to catch him.

He answered on the second ring. "Aunt Eve!" he exclaimed, his delight transmitting itself over the phone line. "How was the reunion? Did you dazzle 'em?"

Eve could feel much of the evening's tension melting away at the reassuring sound of his voice. "The reunion was fine. And, yes, lots of my old classmates seemed appropriately dazzled."

"I knew they would be. How could they help it?"

"You might be a tad prejudiced, you know."

"Who, me? Just speakin' the truth, ma'am. So what's happening? Are you back home now?"

"No, I'm still in Ohio."

"You are? Well, when're you going home?"

"I'm not sure. I'd planned to leave tomorrow, but tonight I decided to stay on for a few more days. There are still some people I haven't had a chance to spend much time with."

"Sounds like you're having fun, then. That's great. You deserve it."

Eve smiled. What a terrific kid he was. It had hurt her Saturday night to hear Mitch brag about his other son and know that he would never know he had more than one terrific kid.

Now stop that! You can't afford to start thinking like this. Oh, God. What was wrong with her? For years she'd been extremely careful not to even think of Matthew as *her* child, let alone Mitch's. It was a luxury she could not afford, and nothing that had happened in the past few days changed that.

"Have you talked to Mom recently?" Matthew asked. A note of concern had crept into his voice.

"No, not for a week or so," Eve said. "Why? Is something wrong?"

She could almost hear his shrug as he answered, "I don't know. She just sounded awfully down when I talked to her yesterday."

"Well, you know, Matthew, it's been hard on her since your dad died. She's lonely." Tony's death the previous year from a Vietnam-related cancer had been hard on Eve, too, but at least Eve had a thriving career and was too busy to mope. Besides, Eve had learned at a young age that no matter how bleak things seemed, life does go on.

"I know she's lonely, but she doesn't do anything about it," Matthew said. "It's bad for her to sit around the house so much. She needs to get out and meet people. I told her she should think about going back to college and getting her degree."

It never failed to amaze Eve that Matthew possessed a maturity well beyond his nineteen years. "That's exactly what I told her the last time I went up for the weekend," she said. "So what did she say when you told her that?"

He sighed loudly. "Oh, you know. She's too old and set in her ways. She's not smart enough to compete with all the young people in school. And besides, even if she *did* get her degree, who'd want to hire an old woman?"

Eve chuckled at his snort of disgust.

"For cryin' out loud, she's only fifty! That's not old."

"You're right, of course, but give her some time. Maybe it's too soon to expect that much of her. This is a big adjustment for her, because all she's really known is taking care of the house and your dad and you."

"But dad and I are gone," Matthew remarked with the unarguable logic of youth.

"Tell you what. When I get back to New York, I'll insist that she come down to visit me for a week or so, and I'll work on her."

"Would you?" The relief Matthew felt was evident in his voice.

Once again Eve marveled at his maturity, as well as his sensitivity and compassion. She knew these qualities would serve him well in his chosen field of medicine. She smiled again. She was so proud of him. And there was no reason not to tell him so. "You're a great kid, you know that?"

"Now who's prejudiced?"

"Maybe I am, but it's the truth." She waited a heartbeat, then said softly, "I'm very proud of you, Matthew."

"Hey, the feeling is mutual!"

She knew she had embarrassed him, but after spending the evening with Mitch, it was very important to say the things out loud that she'd been thinking and feeling for days. "I love you," she added over the sudden lump in her throat.

"Ditto," he said.

When they hung up, Eve had tears in her eyes. Matthew was her rock. Her talisman. Her touchstone. The very center of her heart. She could not imagine life without him.

They had always shared a very special relationship. Although he had no idea she was his birth mother, there was an undeniable connection between them.

Matthew had often remarked upon it. "I don't know what it is, Aunt Eve," he'd said, "but I can tell you anything."

And he did. He shared his thoughts, his hopes, his fears and his dreams, and Eve felt privileged to receive these precious confidences.

He praised her often.

"You're the most truthful person I know. I can ask you anything, and I always know you'll give me an honest answer."

Whenever he talked about the honesty between them, Eve had squashed her guilty feelings. She *was* honest with him, she told herself. The one secret she'd kept was kept with his best interest at heart, not to shield herself. But even as she rationalized her actions, she couldn't prevent the tiny frisson of fear that wormed its way into her soul. What would happen to her relationship with Matthew if he ever discovered that it was built on a lie?

She always pushed the thought away quickly.

He would never find out.

The only two people still alive who knew the truth were Mary Ann and Eve. And Mary Ann would never tell him. Just the opposite, in fact. Mary Ann would move heaven and earth to keep Matthew from finding out his origins.

Eve wasn't sure she still agreed with Mary Ann. Initially she had sincerely felt it really was in Matthew's best interest not to know about her. She wanted him to have the happiest, most secure childhood possible. But now that he was an adult, she thought he could handle the truth. She sighed. Well, what she thought didn't matter. She had promised Tony and Mary Ann she would not tell Matthew, and unless Mary Ann released her from that promise, the secret must be kept.

She was grateful, though, that he felt so close to her. She loved him with an intensity that sometimes scared her. She had felt that way from the first moment she'd set eyes on him.

She smiled, remembering the snowy March night when he'd been born.

Connecticut, nineteen years earlier

"Push, Eve…push!" urged Mary Ann. She squeezed Eve's right hand in encouragement.

"I *am* pushing," Eve said. Sweat rolled off her face as another contraction—the strongest one yet—gripped her. As she'd been instructed, she took a deep breath, held it for the count of ten, then pushed as hard as she could.

"You're doin' great, hon," Betty, one of the nurse-attendants said. "A couple more like that, and the baby'll be out."

"I can see its head," Dr. Warwick said from her vantage point. "It's got lots of black hair!"

The next few minutes seemed like hours, but Eve endured and pushed and did everything she was told, and the moment finally came when the doctor exclaimed, "The baby's out!"

"It's a boy, a beautiful boy," Betty said. She grinned down at Eve. "You did good, hon."

"A boy!" Mary Ann said.

"A boy," Eve whispered, sinking back against the delivery table.

A lusty cry split the air.

Tears filled Eve's eyes.

The birthing room was a beehive of activity for a few minutes as the myriad details that follow a birth were completed.

"Will you look at that?" the doctor said.

"What?" Eve struggled to sit up. Was something wrong?

"Wait, wait," Betty said, pushing her back down. "You can see in a minute. Let us get him cleaned off first."

And then, to the background of admiring sounds from Mary Ann and the nurses and Tony—who had come into the birthing room—an eight-pound, ten-ounce Matthew John DelVecchio was placed in his mother's arms, and Eve got her first glimpse of her extraordinary son.

Her eyes widened. "Oh, my gosh...look at his hair!" With a forefinger, she gently touched the baby's downy head, which was completely covered in silky black hair neatly divided by a streak of pure white that grew just to the right of the center of his forehead. She'd never seen anything like it.

He looked at her solemnly, and even though she knew that newborns can't see, she felt as if he were studying her as intently as she studied him.

He had a beautiful, round face, and he felt solid and warm in her arms. He made tiny little sucking noises, and unexpectedly Eve choked up. A tear slipped down her cheek.

Her son.

She swallowed, too filled with emotion to speak.

Her beautiful son. She smiled through her tears. Her beautiful, *unique* son with his streak of white hair.

In that moment, she knew what it was to feel perfect, unconditional love, and she made a solemn vow. Even though Matthew would never know she was his birth mother, she would always be there for him. No matter what happened in the future, she would never let him down.

To keep from thinking about her feelings concerning Mitch, Eve spent most of Tuesday on the telephone. Her assistant, Chloe Barnett, wasn't happy to find out her boss had decided to stay in Maple Hills a few days longer.

"Did you forget about your appointment with Whitney Shaw?" Chloe asked.

Eve grimaced. Whitney Shaw, by virtue of her four Academy Award nominations, received preferential treatment at DelVecchio Designs. The actress always insisted on a personal appointment with Eve and no one else. "Call and explain that I've been delayed a few days and see if we can't reschedule."

"She's not gonna like it," Chloe warned.

"I know, but it can't be helped."

"And what about Jonathan? Weren't you supposed to go to the theater with him Thursday night?"

Jonathan Douglas was more than just the designer with whom Eve had apprenticed many years ago. He was her mentor and a close personal friend. "Yes, but he'll understand, and I'm sure he can find someone else to take. Actually, I'll call him myself."

"Maybe you'd better call Whitney Shaw, too."

"Now, Chloe . . ."

"I know, I know, it's my job to take care of these unpleasant tasks," Chloe grumbled.

Eve smiled. Chloe loved to blow smoke, but she was a crackerjack assistant, and Eve didn't know what she'd do without her.

"So when *are* you coming home?" Chloe asked after listing several dozen more appointments that would need to be rescheduled or canceled completely and receiving Eve's instructions.

"I'll be back in the office next Monday."

"You promise."

"I promise."

After hanging up, Eve immediately called Jonathan. "Is he in, Rose?" she asked his secretary.

"Oh, hi, Miss DelVecchio. Yes, he's in. Hold on a minute."

"Eve, darling!" Jonathan said when they were connected. "You're back!"

"No, Jonathan, I'm not. I'm still in Ohio."

"Whatever for?"

Eve grinned. Jonathan was a native New Yorker, and it was his opinion that anything west of Philadelphia was the wilderness. She could just imagine the look of distaste flitting across his elegant face. "There are some old friends here that I want to spend a little more time with, so I'm afraid I won't be home until next week."

"But we have a date for Thursday night," he said crossly.

"I know, and I'm sorry. But you can take someone else."

"No one who's as much fun as you are."

"Now, Jonathan, sweetie, please don't be angry. I can't help it. Truly."

"Well . . ."

Eve smiled. Sometimes Jonathan acted crochety, but he was loyal, discreet, and would give his friends the shirt off his back. She loved him dearly.

They talked for a while longer, with Jonathan telling her the latest gossip in fashion circles and Eve making all the right comments in return. Finally, when Eve felt her old friend was appropriately placated, she said goodbye.

Afterward she decided she would take a long, leisurely bath in preparation for her evening with Mitch. She filled the tub with bath salts and steaming water, then lowered herself in, laid her head back and closed her eyes.

Immediately, all the thoughts, all the doubts she'd managed to keep at bay throughout the day deluged her.

She shouldn't have agreed to stay in Maple Hills. She shouldn't have agreed to have dinner with Mitch tonight. Seeing him again was crazy. She'd been right when she'd told him there was no point to it. In fact, there was every reason in the world *not* to see him again. Being with him was dangerous, because contrary to what she'd told herself before coming back to Maple Hills, she couldn't easily dismiss him as unworthy of attention.

There's no harm in just having dinner with him.

Ha! Who was she kidding? After what had transpired between them last night, Mitch had more on his mind than dinner. And she was obviously not capable of resisting.

You don't want to resist.

Eve sank lower in the tub as if she could somehow escape her thoughts.

In fact, if he hadn't stopped making love to you when you so halfheartedly told him to, you'd probably have let him undress you right out there in the gardens. That's how much willpower you have when it comes to Mitchell Sinclair.

Eve swallowed.

Oh, God. Was she that weak? That stupid? Could a few kisses and a few words of apology just erase all the pain he'd caused her?

No, but if it hadn't been for Mitch, you wouldn't have Matthew, now would you?

She sighed. At the root of everything was that one undeniable truth. How could she regret the time with Mitch? How could she regret the lovemaking that had resulted in her magnificent son? How could she even regret the pain, when the pain was a part of it all?

Okay, so she didn't. But not regretting the past was one thing. Taking up with Mitch again was another.

But why shouldn't I go out with him? In fact, why shouldn't I make him want me again? What's wrong with wanting a little revenge for the way he played so fast and loose with me?

Yes, why shouldn't she go tonight? Why shouldn't she be deliberately charming and captivating and make him want her desperately? Wouldn't it give her an enormous feeling of satisfaction—of closure, even—to build his hopes and then crush him the way he'd crushed her?

You're playing with fire. And people who play with fire usually get burned. If you were smart, you'd get out of this tub right now, go to the phone, call him up and say you've changed your mind. Then you'd get your fanny on the first plane out of here.

Eve opened her eyes and sat up. Slowly she stood. She stepped carefully out of the tub and ignored the water cascading off her body and onto the bathroom tiles.

She wrapped one of the big terry-cloth towels around her sarong-style and headed for the telephone.

Chapter Ten

Mitch left the office early Tuesday afternoon. He'd decided to stop by to see his mother on his way home, and he wanted to be sure he had plenty of time afterward to get ready for his evening with Eve.

It was a bright, beautiful June day with low humidity and a cloudless sky—the kind of day that always made Mitch feel good to be alive. He whistled as he drove toward his parents' home. He cautioned himself against expecting too much tonight, yet he couldn't help the feeling of excitement and anticipation that simmered beneath his calm exterior.

As he rounded the corner from Main Street to State Street, he passed Peggy's Posies, the local florist. Impulsively he pulled into the parking lot.

Peggy Houseman, a freckle-faced dynamo whose son had played on the same soccer team with Nicholas, came out of the back room of the shop when the bell on the front door heralded Mitch's arrival. "Hey, Mitch!" she said. "Good to see you." A wide grin split her face.

"Hi, Peggy. How's it goin'?"

"Just great. Gee, I was sorry to hear about your mother's fall."

"Yeah, she's really upset. You know how she hates inactivity." He grinned. "Of course, we both know what she *really* hates is missing any of the action."

Peggy laughed. "Well, lots of people miss her, too, if the amount of flowers ordered are any indication."

Mitch grimaced. "Are you saying it's a bad idea for me to bring her flowers?"

"Oh, no, I'd never say that. A woman can never have too many flowers."

Mitch eyed the already-prepared bouquets in the refrigerated display case. "How about that one?" He pointed to a tall crystal vase filled with daisies.

"Excellent choice," Peggy said. She removed the chosen arrangement. "Most of the people who've sent her arrangements have sent plants, so this'll be a nice change."

Mitch had already handed Peggy his credit card when he spied the violets. A thick cluster of velvety blooms in a pale blue porcelain vase, they were delicate and irresistibly lovely, just like the equally delicate and irresistibly lovely woman he would see tonight.

"I'll take those violets, too," he said.

"Wow, your mother's a lucky woman to have such a generous son."

Mitch thought about not correcting Peggy's assumption that the violets were for his mother. Did he really want the town gossiping and speculating about him? On the other hand, he had nothing to hide, did he? This time around, he was perfectly free to court Eve Del-Vecchio.

"The violets are for someone else," he said. "Is it still possible to get them delivered this afternoon?"

"You're in luck. Ordinarily Skip would already be gone on his last delivery, but he's running late today. He just called to say he's on his way back to pick up the last couple of orders. Where do you want this one to go?"

"To Eve DelVecchio at the Maple Hills Inn."

To Peggy's credit, she didn't say anything except, "All right. Here's a card you can sign." She began to ring up his purchases.

He accepted the card, thought for a minute, then wrote, I'm looking forward to tonight. Love, Mitch. He made sure he sealed the envelope tightly.

Fifteen minutes later he pulled into his parents' driveway.

"Oh, Mitch, the flowers are beautiful!" his mother said as he walked into the family room where she was ensconced in his father's recliner, her casted leg propped high with pillows. "Thank you."

Mitch bent down and kissed her cheek. She smelled of White Linen, the perfume she'd worn forever. "How are you feeling?"

She sighed. "Oh, I feel all right, just frustrated because I'm stuck here in this house for heaven knows how long." She looked at the flowers. "Why don't you put them over there on the desk in front of the window?"

"Okay."

Stella Masucci, the woman who had been their household help ever since Mitch was a child, poked her head around the corner from the kitchen. "Hello, Mitch."

Mitch looked up and smiled. "Hi, Stella. How are you?"

"Just great."

"And how's Connie?" Mitch asked, naming Stella's oldest daughter, who had gone to high school with him.

"Expecting her fourth next month," Stella said proudly.

"Four. Wow." Mitch suppressed a twinge of envy.

"Stella's coming every afternoon now that I'm laid up," his mother said.

Mitch nodded. "Dad told me." He didn't need to ask where his father was. Ever since Clifford Sinclair had retired, he could be found at the country club golf course nearly every afternoon.

The three of them talked a few more minutes, then Stella said, "Well, Mrs. Sinclair, I'm leaving now. The chicken and rice and green beans are all cooked and ready to eat. All Mr. Sinclair will have to do is heat them in the microwave. And there's a salad and a lemon meringue pie in the fridge."

"Thanks, Stella. I'll see you tomorrow," Pamela said.

Stella left, and Pamela turned to Mitch. "People have really been so nice. I've already had tons of visitors. That fruit basket is from my bridge club, those roses came from Eve DelVeccio and Ann Marie Flynn stopped by this afternoon. She brought me those mixed nuts...oh, and she told me about last night's dinner party."

Mitch suppressed a grimace. He had hoped his mother wouldn't know about last night.

Pamela's eyes were bright with curiosity. "Tell me all about it. How did Eve DelVeccio look and what did she wear and what's she like?"

Mitch sat on the couch and helped himself to a handful of cashews. "She looked like a typical success-ful New Yorker," he said casually, "all dressed in black and diamonds. Sophisticated and beautiful."

Pamela nodded. "Was she nice, or did she act snooty?"

"She was very nice."

"Well, come on, tell me everything. What did she have to say? Did she mention me?"

"Yes, as a matter of fact, she did. She mentioned that you'd called her and how sorry she was that you'd had an accident."

Pamela frowned. "Not half as sorry as me."

"Well, it could have been worse. At least you can walk if you need to."

"Yes, I guess you're right."

"So what have you been doing with yourself all day? Do you need something to read?" Mitch was glad they'd changed the subject. Talking about Eve was too dangerous. There was too much chance he'd say something he shouldn't.

"I've got plenty of books and things to do. Actually, today I went through old photos. I've been wanting to put together an album for Nicholas...you know... something that will give him a record of his ancestors."

Mitch smiled. "That's a great idea."

She reached over to a nearby table. "Look. I've already started."

Mitch took the proffered album. A label on the outside proclaimed it to be the family album of Nicholas Clifford Sinclair. Mitch turned to the first page. He smiled, recognizing the old sepia-tinted photograph. "Great-great grandfather Emerson, right?"

"Yes."

Mitch studied the photograph. "Boy, Nicholas is really a throwback, isn't he?"

His mother smiled, her eyes softening. "No doubt about it. He's all Emerson."

Mitch continued leafing through the album, pausing when he saw the eight-by-ten print of his and Carolyn's wedding picture. He remembered how he hadn't wanted any photographs taken but how he hadn't said anything when Carolyn had insisted on them.

He stared at their likenesses. He looked solemn in his dark suit and white shirt. Actually he'd been in a state of shock, still not sure how he'd ended up there. Carolyn, on the other hand, looked triumphant in her short white lace dress and veil. As well she should, he thought wryly.

"Here comes your father," Pamela said, interrupting Mitch's thoughts.

Mitch looked up as his father entered through the back door.

"Hello, son," Clifford Sinclair said.

"Hi, Dad."

His father walked over, leaned down and pecked his wife on the cheek. "How'd your day go?"

"As if you care," she said crossly.

"Now, Pamela..."

"If you *really* cared, you'd have stayed home today," she continued.

His father winked at Mitch over his mother's head. "Now you know that me staying home wouldn't change things, would it? Besides, you weren't alone. Stella was here."

"Oh, don't try to gloss over the fact that your golf game means more to you than I do. I learned that a long time ago.'' She gave Mitch one of her long-suffering looks.

Mitch suppressed a grin and said, ''Well, now that Dad's home, I've got to be going. You take care of yourself, Mom, and stay off that foot.''

''Oh, do you have to leave so soon? Why don't you stay for dinner?'' his mother said. ''Stella always makes more than your father and I can eat.''

''Thanks, but I can't.''

''Oh?'' Her expectant tone and expression told Mitch plainly that she wanted him to elaborate. When he didn't, she persisted, saying, ''Have you got a date?''

''Pamela,'' his father said, ''it's none of your business whether he has a date or not.''

Her face tightened, and she opened her mouth to retort, but Mitch forestalled her by saying, ''I'll call you tomorrow, okay? Now I really do have to take off. Night, Dad. Night, Mom.'' He kissed his mother's cheek, waved in his father's direction, and made his escape.

By five-thirty, Eve still hadn't been able to contact Mitch. As she debated whether or not to keep trying or just to go ahead and get ready for the evening, there was a knock at the door of her suite.

''These flowers were just delivered for you, Miss DelVecchio,'' said Todd, her favorite of the bellhops.

She tipped him generously, thinking whoever had sent the violets had exquisite taste.

Then she read the card. She tried to tamp down her pleasure. She told herself anyone could fashion pretty words. But every time she looked at the violets, she smiled, and a warmth blanketed her heart.

All thought of canceling her dinner date was banished, and she proceeded to get ready for the evening. As she dressed, she was torn between wanting to look conservative and aloof—so as to send him a clear message about where they were *not* going to take their relationship—and wanting to knock his eyes out so he'd desire her more than ever.

She compromised, settling on a forest green crepe dress from her Nature collection. It was fashioned with a high neck, cap sleeves, and petal skirt that just skimmed the tops of her knees. She accessorized her outfit with her aquamarine-and-diamond crescent pin, cream-colored hose and matching pumps.

Once again, she pinned up her hair. Wearing it loose and curly left her feeling less in control, and tonight she knew she needed all the control she could muster.

A few minutes before seven she headed for the lobby.

Mitch, dressed in a charcoal suit that set off his dark blond good looks to perfection, was already there and waiting for her. He walked forward when he saw her get out of the elevator. His eyes, warm and admiring, swept her from head to toe.

Eve's heart skipped a beat as she met his gaze. Why did he have to be so damned attractive? And why did she have to be so damned weak?

"You look sensational," he said softly.

"Thank you." He looked sensational, too, but she certainly wasn't going to tell him so. "Thank you for the flowers, as well. They're lovely."

"Not half as lovely as you are."

She wished he didn't look so sincere. He made it very difficult to maintain the kind of distance she knew it was imperative to maintain.

He smiled down at her and took her elbow to walk her outside. Even that small contact set up a flutter in her breast, which she tried to ignore. The valet parking attendant held the passenger door to Mitch's car open, and Mitch helped her inside. Their gazes met again, and Eve's traitorous heart beat even faster. What was wrong with her? For years, she had prided herself on her ability to control her emotions. In her social circle, she was known as the "Ice Maiden."

But with Mitch, all the gains she'd made in the past twenty years had melted away and she felt completely stripped of defenses.

"I've made reservations at The Treehouse in Berwyn Falls," Mitch said as they pulled away from the hotel. "I hope that's all right with you."

"I've never been to The Treehouse," she said, genuinely pleased, "and I always wanted to go there when I was a kid." The restaurant was so named because it looked like a tree house—built of wood, on pillars, and circled by a thick grove of trees. All dining was on the second level—in one huge room with windows on all sides—and it gave diners the illusion they were floating in the trees. It was a popular place for weddings and wedding receptions.

Mitch tuned the radio to a classical station, and by unspoken agreement, they listened to music on the forty-minute drive to the restaurant and made no attempt at conversation.

Eve was glad of the reprieve. She knew Mitch would want to talk about their relationship, and she wasn't ready for it. Yet by the time they reached the restaurant and were seated at their corner table, she was so tense, all she wanted was to get the conversation over with.

She knew what she had to do. Last night, when she'd tried to tell him a renewal of their relationship would be unwise, she had been right. And if she'd had any doubts at all, her reactions so far tonight had erased them. She could not afford to throw her life into chaos, which is exactly what would result if she attempted to resume a relationship so fraught with complications.

Mitch made it easier to introduce the topic when, after their waiter had taken their drink order, he smiled and said, "I've been thinking about you all day. I couldn't wait for tonight to get here."

Eve did not return his smile. "I almost didn't come." *Get it over with. Tell him.* "I called your office to tell you I'd changed my mind, but you'd already gone for the day. I called your house, too, but there wasn't any answer."

"You didn't leave a message."

"No."

"And you're here now."

"Yes, but I already know it was a mistake."

"Don't say that." He reached across the table and tried to take her hand, but she put her hands in her lap. This would be hard enough without the added pressure of his touch.

"Mitch, I told you last night. There's no point to this. We have no future together, so it would be stupid to start something that can go nowhere."

"But Eve, how do you know—" Mitch broke off as their waiter approached with their wine. While he poured, then waited for Mitch to taste it and give it his okay, Eve worked on getting her emotions on an even keel.

After the waiter left, Mitch leaned forward and said earnestly, "Look, let's not discuss this now. Why not just relax and enjoy the evening? We can save this conversation for later when we have some privacy, okay?''

Eve supposed his suggestion made sense. After all, she was here, and they *were* going to have dinner. And she'd already told him exactly how she felt. She nodded. ''Okay.''

She had to give him credit. He played completely fair, never allowing the subsequent conversation to veer into personal territory. Throughout the evening, he was the most charming, attentive host anyone could have asked for. He kept the conversation flowing—talking about his law practice and a couple of his most interesting cases. Then he asked her about her career, and Eve discovered he was a terrific listener. His questions were intelligent and his grasp of her explanations immediate.

Eve was amazed to find herself relaxing, just as he'd suggested they should.

She only had one bad time during the evening, and that came over dessert when Mitch asked about her family, after bringing her up to date on his.

''I know your parents are dead,'' he said. ''I saw the notices in the paper.''

''Yes. I miss them a lot.''

''They were good people.''

''Yes, they were.''

''What about your brother? Does he still live in Connecticut?''

Eve shook her head sadly. ''Tony died of cancer last year.''

''Oh, I'm sorry, Eve. I know how hard it is to lose a brother you love,'' he said softly.

''It was terrible. He was only fifty-two. Far too young.''

After a few minutes of sympathetic silence, he said, "So you have no family left at all."

"Only my sister-in-law—Tony's wife, Mary Ann— and...and their son." Now *why* had she stammered like that? Her heart began to thump too hard as she realized how tenuous was her control. For one frightening moment, she was sure Mitch could see right through her. That he could know how vulnerable she suddenly felt.

But he didn't seem to realize there was anything wrong at all. He just smiled and asked, "Are you very close to them?"

"Yes, very." *Oh, God, if you only knew.*

"Good. The older I get, the more I realize how important family is. I know I'm constantly grateful for Nicholas." When he said his son's name, his face immediately lit up with love and pride.

Eve clenched her hands in her lap. She felt ridiculously close to tears. Oh, she was a fine mess if she couldn't even make a casual mention of Matthew or hear a casual mention of Nicholas without falling to pieces. "Do you have a picture of him?" she said to cover her agitation.

Mitch grinned. "Of course." He reached for his wallet, flipped through it, then removed a photo. "Unfortunately, I don't have a recent one. That one was taken last Thanksgiving in Vermont."

Eve took the photo. She stared at the picture of a smiling teenager in a black-and-white ski outfit and red knitted cap. She felt almost lightheaded as she studied his face closely for any resemblance to Matthew. They definitely had the same shaped face, the same nose, but maybe no one but her would think so. Maybe she realized they looked similar because she was looking for similarities. "He looks like you," she finally managed to say. She handed back the picture.

Mitch put it back into his wallet. "He's all Emerson—that's my mother's side of the family." He grimaced. "Boy, I've missed him the past couple of weeks."

"Where is he?"

"In Europe with his grandparents. Didn't I mention that before?"

Eve shook her head. "Not that I remember." Hadn't Carolyn been in Europe with her parents all those years ago? Wasn't that the reason Mitch was free to get involved with Eve in the first place? Well, not exactly free, she thought wryly. In fact, not free at all.

The reminder was like a dash of cold water. And although she really didn't need reinforcement of her decision to say a permanent goodbye to Mitch, her resolve hardened.

No matter what Mitch said later, she would not change her mind. She'd been lucky tonight. He hadn't noticed how flustered and upset she'd become when she'd mentioned Matthew, but if she were to continue to see him, she might not always be so lucky.

And that would be disastrous.

So it was with a great sense of relief that the moment finally came when the evening wound to a close and their waiter brought Mitch the check.

Together they walked out into the balmy summer night. The touch of Mitch's hand resting lightly against her waist, the soft breeze carrying the sweet scent of lilacs, the lilting song of a nightingale perched nearby, and the brilliance of the full moon and star-studded sky all seemed a conspiracy to weaken Eve's determination to keep a clear head and a clearer resolve.

You know what you have to do.

Once again Mitch helped her into the car.

Once again he tuned the radio to classical music.

And once again, quiet settled around them as they drove back to Maple Hills.

As they passed the sign announcing the city limits, Mitch said, "Would you like to see my house? We could go there and have a glass of brandy and talk."

It was so tempting to say yes. She was dying to see where Mitch lived. How he lived. She was dying to see what might have been. How different her life might have become.

She sighed with regret. No matter how much she wanted to say yes, she knew she couldn't indulge her curiosity. It was too risky. "I don't think so, Mitch."

"Oh, come on, Eve. If you're worried about being alone with me, I promise you I won't do anything you don't want me to do. I won't even touch you if it makes you uncomfortable."

"I don't—"

"I'll be a perfect gentleman."

"I—"

"Come on. Say yes. I'll warn you, though, the house is kind of a mess right now. I'm in the middle of re-modeling, so there are tarps everywhere, but I've got a nice porch with a swing. We can sit outside."

Eve thought about going back to her hotel room. She thought about leaving Maple Hills. She thought about never seeing Mitch again.

Oh, for heaven's sake. You're an adult, aren't you? What is the big deal, anyway? You can certainly handle another hour or so in Mitch's company.

"Oh, all right. You talked me into it."

In the muted interior light, she saw his grin. "You won't be sorry."

Chapter Eleven

Mitch's home was nothing like Eve had imagined it would be. Whenever she had thought about him, she had pictured him living in a large brick Colonial like his parents, or a modern split-level in one of the exclusive subdivisions on the outskirts of Maple Hills.

Instead he lived in a pre-World War II, nondescript two-story frame house within walking distance of downtown.

"You're surprised, aren't you?" he said as they pulled into the narrow driveway.

"A little," she admitted. From what he'd told her of Carolyn, she couldn't fathom why the woman would have chosen to live in a house or a neighborhood like this. Although the area wasn't without charm, Eve decided as she looked around.

The trees lining the street were old and stately, the neighborhood was well kept, and Mitch's street backed up to Maple Hills Park, which gave it an attractive wooded setting.

"I bought this house last year." He turned off the ignition but made no move to get out of the car. "I'd always hated the house Carolyn and I lived in together, and besides, I realized both Nicholas and I needed to put the past behind us." He grimaced. "Carolyn's death was hard on him. She might have had her faults, but she was a good mother."

Eve nodded. It must have been awful for Nicholas losing his mother like that.

"The house was in a sad state of disrepair, so I bought it at a good price. I had it cleaned up and the most pressing of the major repair work done—like a new roof and a new furnace and a major plumbing overhaul."

"So what's being done now?"

"Mostly cosmetic things—painting and new carpet, some cabinet work, updating and remodeling of the bathrooms—things to make the house more attractive and livable."

As they talked, they got out of the car.

"Watch your step," he said as they walked up the back steps.

They stepped into a screened-in porch, which led directly into the kitchen. Mitch snapped on the overhead light, and Eve looked around curiously. The kitchen was big, bright and inviting. Surprisingly so. The cabinets were a highly polished knotty pine, the countertops and floor white ceramic tile, the wallpaper a cheery red-and-white peppermint stripe, and sitting in the middle of the square room—were a large round maple table and chairs with royal blue cushions. All the accent pieces in the kitchen were either bright red or the same shade of royal blue.

"What a nice kitchen," she said. "It doesn't look in need of remodeling at all."

He grinned. "That's because it's done. It was the first room they worked on. They finished it last month. I'm glad you like it."

"It's wonderful, actually." And the fact that Carolyn had never lived in the house, never touched these counters or prepared a meal here, made it even more wonderful.

"If you like, I'll show you around the rest of the downstairs before we have our drink."

"I'd love to see the rest."

The balance of the first floor contained a nicely proportioned living room with a fireplace, a dining room with window seats, a powder room that Mitch explained had until recently been a full bath, and two bedrooms—one that Mitch had made into an office and one that was a cozy TV room.

"This is where Nicholas and his friends hang out," Mitch said.

All the floors and most of the furniture were covered with tarps, just as Mitch had warned, and the whole place smelled of fresh paint and new carpeting.

There were no pictures, knickknacks or small articles laying about. Obviously everything small had been packed away while the workmen were there.

"Everything upstairs is a mess," he said, "except for my bedroom, which I insisted they finish first. Basically, there are three bedrooms up there—mine, Nicholas's and a guest room. There used to be a huge bathroom up there, too, but I had it divided into two smaller ones so that Nicholas and I don't have to share. And that's pretty much it, except for the basement.''

Eve could see that the house would be charming when it was finished. And oddly, even though she wouldn't have thought so before, she could see that it suited Mitch.

"Ready for that drink now?" he asked.

"Yes."

"While all this work is going on, I've moved the bar supplies to the kitchen, so let's go back there.''

Eve leaned against the kitchen counter and watched as he opened a cupboard, extracted a bottle of brandy and filled two snifters with about an inch of liquid. He handed her one, then inclined his head toward the back porch. "We can sit out there or we can go out front and sit on the swing.''

"I vote for the swing." Eve also voted for street-lights. It was a pretty sad commentary on her state of mind that she felt she needed their protection.

A few minutes later, carefully seated about a foot apart, they swung gently and sipped their brandy. His arm was draped casually along the back of the swing.

Eve decided she would wait for Mitch to initiate the subject of their relationship. After all, she'd already had her say.

She didn't have to wait long.

"What do I have to do to convince you to give me another chance?" he said.

She hadn't expected such directness, and it disconcerted her. She decided to be just as direct. "You know, Mitch, there's a passage in the Bible that says, 'to everything, there is a season.'" She looked up. His eyes gleamed in the darkness. "I think we must face the fact that our season has passed."

He carefully set his glass of brandy on the little wrought-iron table next to the swing, then, as he had last night, he cupped her chin, moving closer in the process. "Is that so?"

She swallowed, willing her heart to calm down. She had nothing to fear. He had promised he would do nothing she didn't want him to do. "You know it is."

His gaze fastened on her mouth. "Oh, Lord, I love your mouth. It was made for kissing."

Unbidden and unwelcome, desire spiraled deep inside, and her breath caught.

"I want to kiss you," he whispered.

Oh, God.

"Do you want me to?" His mouth was only inches away.

Eve's heart was pounding so hard she was sure he could hear it. "N-no," she finally managed to say. "No, I don't."

He smiled. "Liar." With his thumb, he stroked her cheek, then slowly let his thumb brush over her lips. His voice was a low, seductive murmur. "I want to kiss you, over and over again, until both of us are aching for each other." His fingers trailed down, tracing her jawline, then to the hollow in her neck where her pulse beat wildly.

Still holding her gaze, he whispered, "Then I want us to go inside, upstairs to my room, and I want to undress you, and I want you to undress me, and then, slowly, I want us to make love. I want to touch you...everywhere. I want to show you how good it can be between us...even better than it was when we were young."

Eve sat mesmerized, unable to move, her mind fastening on the images he'd conjured, while inside, all kinds of things were happening to her body—things that were going to make it very difficult to continue resisting him. From somewhere, she summoned enough strength to say, "S-stop it, Mitch."

"Stop what? Stop talking? Or stop touching you?"

"Everything. Stop everything. I—I want to go home." Abruptly she stood, forgetting about the brandy in the glass she still held. Some of the liquid sloshed over the side and down the front of her dress. "Oh, see what you've made me do!" She was very near tears.

He immediately stood. "Oh, Eve, I'm sorry. Come in the house. If we put cold water on that, maybe we can get it out." He reached for her arm.

"Don't touch me!" The tears were going to spill any minute. What was wrong with her? Why did she let him affect her this way? *You knew better. You should never have come here. When people play with fire, they get burned.* "I said I want you to take me home." She completely forgot that she'd foolishly thought about making him want her, then rejecting him. All she wanted was to escape.

He sighed. "Okay. Here. Give me your glass."

Fighting the tears, furious with him but more furious with herself, she handed it to him without looking at him.

He put down the glass, then walked to the front door and locked it. "C'mon. We can go this way." He inclined his head toward the front steps.

She allowed him to hold her arm as they navigated the steps, but as soon as they were on the driveway, she shook him free. She marched to the passenger side of his car and waited for him to open it.

He walked up beside her but didn't move.

Open the damned door! she wanted to scream. She was perilously close to losing all control of herself, and she'd die if that happened.

He touched her arm. She closed her eyes. *Please, Mitch, please open the door.*

"I know I've upset you, and I'm very sorry," he said.

"It's okay," she muttered. *Please, please don't be nice to me.*

"It's not okay. I told myself tonight that I would never hurt you again and yet I have. I know I'll probably never see you again, and somehow, I'll have to live with that, but I have to say this. I—I love you, Eve. I've always loved you. I just want you to know that."

The words thrummed in the air between them.

The tears she'd tried so hard to suppress rolled down her face, and she choked back a sob.

"Oh, Eve, sweetheart . . . don't . . . please don't cry."

And then she flung herself into his arms, and he was kissing her, saying her name over and over again, and she was kissing him back. The salty tang of her tears mixed with the sweet, pungent flavor of the brandy they'd drunk, but all Eve really tasted was Mitch, as desire flamed to life, sweeping away all reason and all thought of tomorrow.

Eve had had other lovers over the years, but tonight, with Mitch, she realized anew how different lovemaking could be when more than just physical desire was involved.

Although Mitch tried to slow them down, their need of each other was too great, and after the frantic kissing in the driveway, they hurried into the house, barely making it upstairs before they were pulling and tugging at each other's clothing.

They fell onto the bed. There were no words exchanged, only gasps and moans and a few muttered oaths from Mitch when the condom he tried to put on flew out of his fingers and hit the bedpost.

Eve started to giggle. She couldn't help it. And then Mitch began to laugh. They rolled around on the bed, laughing, until he pinned her under him and said, "This isn't funny. If I don't get the damned thing on..."

"I guess I'd better help you," she said.

The laughing had calmed them down enough so that as they resumed their lovemaking, they were able to take it slower.

"You're so beautiful," he whispered, pressing his mouth against her neck, then slowly moving it over her body.

Eve closed her eyes and allowed herself to float in the warmth of his touch, his kisses and his whispered endearments. He was a wonderful lover, considerate, sweet, gentle and then slowly, gradually, as his control slipped, more demanding, his kisses more insistent, his breathing harsher.

Her body quickened, opening beneath him as he filled her. And it was then, in that moment that their two bodies were joined, before the physical sensations blurred everything else, that she knew she had never gotten over him. She knew that even though she'd only been seventeen when they'd first loved each other, she'd been right.

They belonged together.

This was always how it was meant to be.

Her flesh and his flesh, her heart and his heart, her soul and his soul—together so that the lines between each disappeared—and they became one.

She cried out once, just as he brought her to a shattering peak, and then she allowed herself to topple over the edge into a universe that exploded around her.

"Man, sex sure makes me hungry," Mitch said.

Eve grinned, and his heart lifted. He loved her smile. He'd always loved her smile.

"I never realized what a greedy person you are," she said, eyes twinkling.

He nipped at her ear. "You ain't seen nothin' yet," he whispered.

They were lying together in his big four-poster bed, spoon fashion. He held her close, one hand lazily cupping her breast, the other resting against her stomach. He felt sated, for now, but he knew he would make love to her again. In fact, he longed to touch that tantalizing place that lay so near, but he knew if he did, he wouldn't be able to keep from slipping his fingers inside her warmth, and right now it was better to build his anticipation by denying himself.

She sighed as he gently stroked her, arching her back almost imperceptibly.

Gently he turned her in his arms. "Food can wait," he said just before her mouth opened under his.

Later, after he'd fixed them cinnamon toast and mugs of hot chocolate, they sat in his kitchen—Mitch dressed in a pair of shorts and Eve wrapped in a big white terrycloth robe and looked at each other.

"We have to talk about this," Eve finally said.

For a second, fear clouded his eyes. Then, half-laughing, he said, "Eve, don't scare me like that. For a minute there, I thought you were getting ready to say nothing had changed."

"I could hardly say that, because obviously something *has* changed," she said. Now that she'd had a little time to think about it, she realized that even though she and Mitch had always been destined for each other, that didn't mean there weren't some serious problems.

Like the fact that, if she and Mitch were to try to build any kind of future together, she would have to tell him about Matthew or their relationship would be based on a lie. And right now, she couldn't do that.

She might never be able to do that.

He reached for her hands, clasping them firmly. "Look," he said. "I love you. I've always loved you. I made the biggest mistake of my life when I let you get away, an even bigger one than getting involved with Carolyn. I never thought I'd get a second chance, but now that I have, I don't intend to let you go."

Oh, Mitch.

"Do you love me?" he asked.

She loved his eyes—the clear brown irises, the little gold flecks, the long eyelashes that curled so irresistibly. Those eyes studied her intently. She sighed deeply. "Yes, I love you. God help me, but I do."

He smiled. "Then we can work things out. Somehow we'll work things out."

If only it were that simple. If only I could be completely truthful with you. "It sounds so easy when you say it."

"It will be easy. You'll see."

"What about the fact that I live and work in New York, and you live and work here?"

"Those are just logistics," he said reasonably. "Logistics can be solved."

"Nicholas isn't a logistic. What if he doesn't like me?"

"He'll love you."

"I don't know how you can be so sure."

"How could he help but love you?"

"Mitch..."

"Look, he's been encouraging me to date. In fact, he told me a few months ago that he thought I needed to get married again."

Eve swallowed. Married. Did she want that? Fear crept along her spine.

Their gazes met.

"We don't have to settle anything right now," Mitch said. "I know you're skeptical and probably more than a little scared. Hell, I'm scared, too."

"Are you?"

He nodded. "For now, though, just promise that you'll give us a chance. Let's take things slow. Spend lots of time together. Get to know each other again. Then get you and Nicholas together and see how the two of you jell. And then, well, then we'll talk about the future...okay?"

Could she do this?

Could she grab for this chance at happiness, despite the past?

Of course, right now Mitch wasn't asking for any kind of permanent commitment. He was only asking that they give themselves some time.

She could do that.

After all, the damage was already done. And she wasn't the kind of person who could make love one night and walk away the next.

"Okay," she said.

"That's my girl."

* * *

Eve insisted on going back to the hotel. "I can't spend the night here, Mitch, no matter how much I might like to. I don't want your neighbors talking about me or speculating about the two of us. What if someone should mention something to Nicholas?"

He sighed. "You're right. I'll take you back."

They arrived at the Maple Hills Inn about two o'clock. Mitch had given Eve a shopping bag filled with newspapers to hold in front of her dress because she didn't want anyone seeing the accident she'd had.

He insisted on seeing her to her suite.

But he didn't give her an argument when she kissed him good-night in the open doorway. "Get a good night's sleep and dream of me," he murmured.

"Maybe I'll dream of one of my other lovers," she teased.

"Who is he? I'll kill him."

She chuckled.

"I love it when you laugh," he said. "I love it when that cool facade slips away and I see the real Eve underneath." He looked deep into her eyes. "It's going to work for us this time. I know it is."

"I hope so."

"You know why I think it's going to work?"

She shook her head.

"Because this time we're starting out the right way. We're being totally honest with each other." He kissed the tip of her nose. "Let's always be honest with each other. Okay?"

Long after he'd gone home, Eve lay in bed and wondered if he'd noticed that she had not echoed his promise.

Chapter Twelve

Although Mitch had only had four hours of sleep when the alarm went off at six-thirty Wednesday morning, he felt terrific.

He whistled as he shaved, sang through his shower and hummed while he got dressed. He couldn't remember having such a sense of well-being in a long, long time.

Every time he thought about Eve, he smiled. He couldn't wait to talk to her. He couldn't wait to see her again. He wondered how long she would stay in Maple Hills. Last night, they hadn't had a chance to discuss it. He hoped he could talk her into staying until Nicholas got home. He felt they needed at least that much time to really get to know each other again.

Plus—he might as well be honest with himself—despite what had happened between them last night, he didn't feel at all secure about their relationship. He was afraid that if she went back to New York before he'd convinced her they belonged together—permanently— she would start having doubts again.

He wished he didn't have to go to work today. He wished they could spend the day together. Actually, what he'd really like was for them to spend several days together, without having to say goodbye at night.

As he drove to the office, an idea formed.

He concluded that the smartest thing he could do to cement his relationship with Eve would be to take her away somewhere.

The idea excited him. It was perfect. A few days in Mexico, maybe. Or the Caribbean. Somewhere completely different, where no one knew them, and they could be together every day and every night.

Right now was a perfect time, too. Nicholas was away. The remodeling was close to being finished, and Mitch was sure he could get his secretary to check on the workmen each day. As far as his law practice went, he'd finished the Medlock contracts yesterday and sent them over for Steven Medlock to look at. Nothing else was pressing. He had no cases on the docket. In fact, his next trial was not scheduled until August. This wasn't unusual. Summer was always a slow time for the courts, because judges liked taking vacations just like everyone else.

By the time Mitch reached his office, he had even rehearsed several arguments in case Eve raised objections to his plan. He chuckled as he realized he was acting like a typical lawyer.

Ten minutes later, when Jill arrived, he told her to cancel all his appointments for the rest of the week.

"All of them?" she said.

"Yes. I'm going away for a few days. I need a break." He smiled at her. "You can take the rest of the week off, too."

"But I'm saving my vacation for next month."

"Who said you had to use vacation time?" Mitch said, feeling magnanimous. "Of course, I will need a small favor in exchange."

"How small?"

"I want you to drop by the house both tomorrow and Friday afternoon to check on the workmen. And I'd like to give them your number to call, just in case they run into problems."

"Hey, what a deal," Jill said happily.

Pleased with himself, Mitch picked up the phone and punched in the number of his travel agent.

Eve stretched and yawned.

She felt deliciously drowsy and terribly decadent for lying about in bed when it was obviously so late in the morning, if the sun pouring in through the open drapes was any indication.

She looked at the digital clock on the bedside table— 10:27. She couldn't remember the last time she'd slept this late.

It didn't matter, though. She had no urgent engagements. No reason to have to get up. She could lie here as long as she liked.

Memories of last night drifted through her mind as she turned on her side and snuggled deeper into her pillow.

Last night had been incredible.

Eve knew she was considered beautiful, and she'd always had a lot of self-confidence about the way she looked. At times, she'd even felt sexy and desirable.

But she'd never felt the way she had last night.

She sighed with deep contentment.

Mitch had made her feel like the most beautiful, most desirable, most sexy woman in the world. He'd also awakened passions that had lain dormant for a long time. She smiled. And he'd been so right...making love when they were kids couldn't compare with how good it had been between them last night.

Their lovemaking was so good it had frightened her. She'd never considered herself superstitious, but she couldn't help feeling that anything that gave her that much pleasure might be taken away.

Don't think like that.

But how could she help it? Especially considering the last thing Mitch had said to her about the new honesty between them. She resolutely pushed the thought away. She didn't want anything to interfere with her happiness this morning. Besides, there wasn't a blasted thing she could do about the situation. So why worry?

She stretched again. She should call and order coffee and think about getting up. Rolling over, she reached for the phone, and as she did, it rang.

"Hello?"

"Good morning. Did I wake you?"

Mitch's voice was low and intimate, causing a shivery sensation to prickle at the back of her neck and warmth to curl into her belly. "Good morning. No, you didn't wake me. I was just going to call down to room service for coffee." She smiled lazily. "I'm still in bed, though."

He made a sound like a moan. "Don't do that."

"Do what?"

"You know what."

Eve laughed. "Where are you? At home?"

"Nope. I was a good boy. I came to work at eight o'clock, just like every morning."

"I'm proud of you."

"You should be, because what I really wanted to do was come over to the hotel and climb into bed with you and commit unspeakable acts."

"Unspeakable acts? Really? That sounds interesting." She gave an exaggerated sigh. "Too bad you have to work today."

"Well, actually...speaking of work...I had an idea this morning."

"Oh?"

"I'm in good shape here at the office. Nothing critical, nothing that can't wait a few days. In fact, I've, uh, arranged to take tomorrow and Friday off. What would you think about the two of us going away somewhere for a few days?"

"Oh, Mitch, that sounds wonderful. What exactly did you have in mind?"

He chuckled. "Sand, sun, margaritas..." He lowered his voice. "Sex."

"Is that all you men think about?" she teased.

"What else is there?" Then he laughed. "Seriously, going away would give us some breathing space...time to really get to know each other again."

"Oh, let's!" she said. "And I know the perfect place. I've got a house at Martha's Vineyard. You'll love it there. It's wonderful."

There was a slight hesitation before he answered. "Look, Eve, don't take this the wrong way, okay? I promise you that I don't have a problem with your success...or your money...and in the future, I'd love to spend time with you in Martha's Vineyard or anywhere else, but right now, this one time, it's important for me to do this."

His words took some of the edge off her euphoria and reminded her that perhaps they might have more than one problem standing in their way. "I understand," she said slowly.

"Do you?"

"Yes." And she did.

"Besides," he added, "I'd like to go someplace where we'd have real privacy. Where no one knows you . . . or me. That way we can be completely relaxed . . . and not have to worry about what other people might think or say."

"You're right."

"How about the Caribbean? My travel agent recommended a small hotel on the island of Saint James. She says it's fairly secluded and really beautiful, and they have private bungalows. I, uh, took the liberty of reserving one, just in case."

"Pretty sure of yourself, weren't you?"

"Hopeful."

"Oh, Mitch, it sounds wonderful. When did you want to leave?"

"There's a flight to Miami that leaves at one-thirty. Can you be ready?"

"One-thirty! Good heavens, it's already ten forty-five! But I guess I can make it."

"Great. I'll pick you up at noon."

Eve took the fastest shower she'd ever taken, tied her wet hair back into a ponytail, threw on a pair of jeans, a navy-and-white-striped T-shirt, and her sneakers, then hurriedly packed. Unfortunately, the clothing she'd brought to Ohio wasn't going to be all that practical for the beach—in fact, she hadn't even brought a bathing suit with her—but surely she could buy one in Saint James.

By eleven-thirty, she had everything ready to go. She called down at the bell desk, then called her assistant.

"Chloe? Change of plans. I'm going down to the Caribbean for a few days. But I still plan to be in the office on Monday."

"The Caribbean? What's going on? What happened to spending time with friends in Ohio?"

"I told you. I changed my plans."

"This isn't like you, Eve. You don't do anything on the spur of the moment."

"I'll tell you all about it when I get back. I promise."

"It's a man, isn't it?" Chloe said. "It's gotta be a man. Anytime a woman acts so completely out of character, there's always a man involved."

Eve smiled. "You're too smart for your own good, Barnett."

"Eve! Who *is* he?" Chloe's voice was practically a squeal.

"Just a man I knew as a kid."

"Just a man you knew as a kid! He must be some kind of guy for you to go traipsing off to the Islands with him."

"Listen, Chloe, I really don't have time to talk right now. He's picking me up in less than twenty minutes, and I've got a couple of other calls to make. I'll see you Monday, okay?"

"Wait! Aren't you going to give me a number where I can reach you?"

"No."

"Eve!"

"The world won't fall apart if I'm incommunicado for a few days. You'll take care of everything beautifully. I know you will."

"I think I want a raise," Chloe said grumpily.

"How much?"

"Five hundred dollars a month."

"That's extortion."

"Hey, *you're* the one who wants to go on some romantic hideaway vacation, and *I'm* the one stuck here taking care of everything."

Eve grinned. "Good point. Five hundred it is." Then, laughter bubbling over in her voice, she said, "You should have asked for more. I would've gone for a thousand."

She was still chuckling when she placed her second call to Jamie. "Just wanted to say goodbye before I left," she said.

"But I thought you left yesterday!" Jamie said.

"I decided to stay on an extra day."

"Well, it was wonderful to see you again, Eve. This time, let's stay in touch, okay?"

"Exactly what I was thinking. In fact, I'd like for you and Bob to come to New York and visit me. The kids, too, if you want to bring them along."

"Oh, Eve! That would be so much fun! I'd love to."

"Good. We'll plan on it. I'll call you in a week or two and we'll firm up a date."

After they hung up, Eve girded herself for the final call. The phone rang five times before her sister-in-law answered.

"Hello." Mary Ann's voice sounded listless.

"Mary Ann? Hi! This is Eve."

"Oh, hi, Eve." She said it with no enthusiasm.

"How are you?"

"Fine."

"You sound tired."

"I was sleeping."

Sleeping? It was almost noon. "I talked to Matthew the other day."

"Did you?" Still no enthusiasm.

Eve decided to be blunt. "He's worried about you." Silence.

Eve's voice softened. "Mary Ann, you've got to snap out of this."

"You don't understand."

"I *do* understand, but this moping about isn't good for you."

Mary Ann's voice hardened. "Look, Eve. What do you want from me—blood? I'm not you. I'm not strong like you are." Her voice broke. "Oh, God, I miss Tony so much. This house is so empty without him."

All Eve's impatience and exasperation disappeared into a wave of sympathy. "Oh, sweetie, I know. Listen, you need a change of scenery." She forced herself to speak brightly. "I know what. Come to New York next week."

"Thanks, Eve, but I don't think so."

"Please, Mary Ann. It'll do you good to get away. And we'll have fun together. We'll go out to lunch, see some shows, go shopping. I'll treat you to a day at Elizabeth Arden—the works."

"I—"

"I won't take no for an answer. It's settled. I'll be back in the office on Monday. I'll look for you on Tuesday."

Mary Ann finally agreed, and they said their goodbyes just as the bellboy arrived to take Eve's bags downstairs.

Eve decided to relegate further thoughts of Mary Ann to the back of her mind. For now, all she wanted to think about was Mitch and the promise of the four wonderful days stretching ahead of them.

Eve's first view of Saint James fulfilled all her expectations. Verdant green hills, red-roofed buildings, bougainvillea and hibiscus and jasmine spilling from every nook and cranny, smiling natives speaking in a lilting cadence, the shimmering aquamarine waters of the Caribbean, and everywhere the golden touch of the sun.

She nestled into the crook of Mitch's arm and smiled up at him.

"Happy?" he said.

"Very."

Their taxi driver got them to the Jewel of the Sea Inn in record time. As he pulled up to the two-story white stucco building tucked into a lush backdrop of palm trees and exotic plants interspersed with a riot of flowers in every conceivable shade of scarlet, purple and pink, Eve said, "Oh, Mitch, this is perfect."

Thirty minutes later, they were shown to their bungalow—the last one on the winding path that climbed behind the hotel. Facing the sea, it sat in a secluded spot on top of a low rise.

The bungalow consisted of a large bedroom, an equally large living room, a tiny kitchenette, a bathroom and a little terrace.

When they were finally alone, Mitch took her into his arms. "I've been wanting to do this for hours," he said, kissing her hungrily.

A long time later, Mitch said, "Well, now that we've christened the bed, how about food? I'm starving."

Eve pretended to be hurt. "What? I'm not enough for you? You want food, too?"

He threw a pillow at her and they ended up having a glorious, giddy pillow fight. Eve couldn't believe she was acting like this. If her friends could see her, they wouldn't believe it, either.

When they finally settled down again, Eve said, "You know, in New York I'm known as the Ice Maiden."

Mitch idly traced her collarbone. "Really?"

"Yes, really." She captured his hand, raising it to her lips and kissing it. "You're good for me, Mitch. You make me forget about myself." She smiled into his eyes. "I do love you."

His eyes softened. And just before he kissed her, he whispered, "Not half as much as I love you."

"That one," Mitch said.

"I don't know," Eve said doubtfully. She fingered the maillot. "I never wear red." She reached for a pale blue suit.

"Please humor me," Mitch said, removing the blue suit from her hands and putting it back. "We'll take the red," he told the smiling salesclerk.

While the clerk rang up Eve's purchases—several pairs of shorts and T-shirts, a pair of sandals, and the bathing suit with accompanying mesh cover-up—Mitch whispered in Eve's ear. "I'm getting excited just thinking about you in that red suit."

She grinned.

Purchases paid for, they walked out of the shop into the bright morning sunlight.

They spent the rest of morning on the beach. Mitch had been right about the red suit. She looked sensational in it. At first, he'd wanted her to buy a bikini, but now he was glad she'd insisted on the maillot. Actually, the suit, cut high on her hips, was sexier than any bikini he'd ever seen. The fabric clung to her slender body, lovingly hugging each curve, and every time Mitch looked at her, he wanted her more.

He wasn't sure he'd ever get enough of her, he decided late that afternoon after they'd finally come indoors—replete with sun and sand and ready for a siesta and other delights.

About six, they got up and showered, then dressed for the evening. Mitch put on a pair of loose white cotton pants and an open-necked brown cotton shirt, and Eve wore a tangerine cotton sundress with her new sandals. Hand in hand, they walked slowly down the path to the hotel.

After a leisurely seafood dinner and several margaritas each, they headed out to the terrace where a trio of island musicians played lilting, subtly seductive music.

"I love dancing with you," Mitch said as he drew her into his arms. "Why haven't we ever danced much?"

"Because the first time around we spent most of our time assuaging our hormones and making love in your car," she said, laughing up at him.

"Well, I wouldn't want to neglect our hormones this time around, either."

"Fat chance," she said. "Your hormones are *very* insistent."

After that they didn't talk much. Mitch held her close and breathed in the fragrance of her hair, and felt the warmth and silkiness of her skin, and told himself he was the luckiest man in the world. He also bargained with God, telling him that if only he would allow things to work out for them this time, Mitch would never ask Him for anything again.

* * *

Eve decided that the three days and four nights she spent with Mitch on Saint James were the most perfect days and nights of her life.

Images were etched into her memory: the lazy days on the beach, walking through the picturesque town, the sunshine and beautiful scenery, the friendly islanders, the long naps in the afternoon, the delicious meals, the romantic evenings filled with music and dancing and a fine, silvery edge of anticipation, and then the nights.

Oh, yes, the nights. Sweet-scented breezes. Soft whispers and slow hands. Heated skin and velvety darkness. Moonlight and magic and mystery. And then, the warmth and safety of Mitch's arms as they slept entwined.

The days slipped by, one by one. Thursday. Friday. Saturday. On Saturday night, after dinner and dancing and an almost bittersweet lovemaking, because each knew it would be their last night there, Mitch stroked her cheek softly and said, "Eve...I want to marry you."

Eve's heart skipped. She stared at him. "I—I don't know what to say."

"You don't have to say anything right now. I just want you to be thinking about it." He kissed her gently, then whispered against her mouth. "I love you so much."

"I love you, too, Mitch, but marriage is a big step."

"I know it is."

"And I haven't even met Nicholas yet."

"I know that, too. I said, just think about it."

She sighed. "All right."

"And promise me you'll keep an open mind."

"I promise."

He kissed her again. "I know there are problems, but we love each other. That's the important thing. All the rest we can work out. I know we can."

Eve wished she shared his optimism. Of course, he didn't know everything she knew. The reminder filled her with disquiet. The past few days had been so perfect, they'd lulled her into a false sense of security. It was one thing to be together on a secluded island; it was quite another to go back to the real world. A world that contained a son Mitch didn't know he had and another son who might or might not like Eve.

"The first thing to do," Mitch said, "is get you and Nicholas together."

"When is he coming home?"

"Next Saturday."

A week from today.

"Can you come back to Maple Hills the following week?" Mitch asked. "I'd bring him to New York, but after being gone so long, I hate to yank him away again."

"No, it's okay. I can come to Maple Hills."

"Good. Just give him a few days to settle in."

"It would be better for me if I came at the end of the week, anyway. How about if I plan to arrive on Friday and stay through Sunday?"

"Well, I wish you'd come earlier, but I understand. I'll have the guest room ready for you."

"No, Mitch, I don't want to stay at your house."

"Why not?"

Eve chose her words carefully. "It's hard to explain, but I know me, and I know I'm going to be nervous and edgy. It's easy for you to say Nicholas will love me, but he may not. I just think it's important to have someplace I can go to be alone and regroup. Besides, your house is Nicholas's turf. I don't want to do anything to make him feel as if I'm crowding him.''

"If that's what you want," he said doubtfully.

"Trust me on this, Mitch.''

"Okay, but I think you're worrying for nothing.''

"I hope so.''

Mitch hugged her. "I know so. Now kiss me, woman. You haven't kissed me for at least ten minutes, and I'm having withdrawal pains.''

Eve did as he asked, but she couldn't turn off her mind. And she couldn't stop worrying.

Mitch made everything sound so uncomplicated. So easy. Eve wanted to believe him. She wanted to believe they could have their second chance. But she couldn't erase her fear. Because she had learned the hard way that everything in life demanded a price. So she could not believe the Fates would let her have Mitch again without extracting payment.

What that payment would be, she could only guess.

Chapter Thirteen

Eve and Mitch flew together to Miami, then, after a lingering kiss and whispered goodbyes, prepared to board their separate flights.

"I'll call you tonight," Mitch promised. He kissed her again, then waved as she reluctantly joined the stream of passengers entering the jetway.

Leaving him was one of the hardest things she'd ever had to do. She couldn't shake the feeling that this glimpse of his tanned, smiling face and sun-bleached hair might be her last. The thought frightened her.

She told herself she was being ridiculous and melodramatic. Of course, she'd see him again. Hadn't they already made the arrangements? She would be back in Maple Hills in less than two weeks. She closed her eyes and tried to sleep, but the closer the plane got to La Guardia and home, the more uneasy she became.

Finally she gave up on sleep and simply stared unseeing out the window and thought about what awaited her in New York. At the root of her uneasiness was the upcoming meeting with Mary Ann.

Sometime during the past few days, Eve had made a decision. She was going to have to tell Mary Ann about Mitch. She was going to have to get her sister-in-law to agree to allow Eve to tell Mitch about Matthew—and vice versa. There was no other way.

Because if Eve wanted to marry Mitch, and she did, she could not continue to keep Matthew's identity a secret from him.

What would Mary Ann say when Eve broached the subject? Could she convince her sister-in-law that "telling the truth" was the right thing to do... indeed, the *only* thing to do, considering recent events?

Eve frowned. She didn't want to, but she couldn't help remembering the one time they had discussed the possibility of Matthew's finding out about his origins.

It had happened a little over a year ago, on his eighteenth birthday. Tony had still been alive, but his cancer had been diagnosed and he was in the midst of aggressive chemotherapy. Still, he'd made an effort to be cheerful and upbeat that day. They all had. They'd decided ahead of time that they would try to make Matthew's birthday as normal as possible because it would probably be the last one where they'd all be together.

Eve leaned her head back and closed her eyes. She remembered the scene vividly.

March 4th, fifteen months earlier

"Think you can manage all those candles?" Eve teased as Matthew bent down and prepared to blow.

"Piece of cake." He grinned, then proceeded to show them.

Just as they had when he was a little tyke, Eve, Tony, Mary Ann and Mary Ann's mother, Lucia, cheered and clapped.

Then they all sat around the dining room table and drank coffee and ate chocolate birthday cake and vanilla ice cream. Afterward Matthew opened his presents.

"Gee, Gran, this is great!" he said as he lifted out the dark green sweater she'd knitted herself. "It'll be perfect for Harvard next year."

Lucia Scarlatti smiled happily.

Matthew was equally enthusiastic and appreciative of his parents' gift—a CD player and gift certificate from a local music store.

Then Eve handed him the tiny box that represented her gift. Mary Ann had been adamantly opposed to Eve's gift when Eve had first introduced the subject, but Tony had overruled her, saying it was perfectly normal for a wealthy relative to buy something more expensive than parents could afford and Matthew would not read anything into it except generosity on his aunt's part.

"Be glad we don't have to worry about going into debt ourselves," he'd said, "cause Matthew's going to need better transportation at college than that old Firebird of his."

"But she's already paying for his education," Mary Ann had replied through stiff lips. "And this house."

"It's the least I can do," Eve had assured her.

Mary Ann had finally relented, and Eve went ahead with her plans. Love pulsed through her as she watched Matthew open the box, part the cotton and lift out the set of keys.

For a moment, his expression was puzzled. Then his hazel eyes met Eve's, and understanding dawned. A look of pure delight lit his face.

Eve grinned. "It's parked next door in the O'Haras' garage."

Matthew let out a whoop, jumped up from the table and enveloped Eve in a bear hug. She hugged him back, and as she did, her gaze met Mary Ann's over his shoulder.

The look in Mary Ann's eyes chilled Eve for a second. It wasn't the first time Eve had felt Mary Ann's resentment. Yet a moment later, Eve told herself she'd imagined the look, because Mary Ann was smiling along with the rest of them as they all trooped outside to see Matthew's new red Honda del Sol convertible.

Later, after Matthew had taken each member of the family for a spin around the block, and Eve had described the chore of getting the car into the O'Hara garage without Matthew seeing it, and Tony had told stories about teaching Matthew how to drive, they were all sitting around the dining room table again. The older members of the family were having second cups of coffee, and Matthew was having a second piece of cake.

Suddenly, out of the blue, Matthew dropped a bombshell. He ate his last bite of cake, put down his fork, looked around the table and said, "Mom, Dad, Gran, Aunt Eve. You ... you all know how much I love you, don't you?"

They all smiled. Eve thought how sweet he was. Most boys his age would have been embarrassed to show open affection, but Matthew had always done so. He'd never been the least bit shy about articulating his feelings and only seemed embarrassed when his family praised him.

"You're the best family in the world. I—I couldn't love you more if we were all flesh-and-blood relatives," he continued.

Goose bumps pricked Eve's arms. It was the first time in a long time that he'd made such an open reference to his adoption, because he knew such remarks bothered his mother. Eve darted a look at Mary Ann. Sure enough, Mary Ann's eyes were filled with dread.

"And I don't want you to take this the wrong way." He reached over and took Mary Ann's hand. "Especially you, Mom," he said softly.

"What is it, Matthew?" Tony said, his voice turning abrupt as it always did when he was upset.

Matthew slowly met each pair of eyes with a look of entreaty. Then he took a deep breath and said, "I—I want your permission to try to find my birth parents."

Eve's heart began to pound, and she didn't know where to look. Finally she looked at Mary Ann, but Mary Ann was staring at Matthew.

"But why, Matthew?" Mary Ann said. "I don't understand."

"It's hard to describe the way I feel, but it's, I don't know...it's kind of like a puzzle...you know...and the critical piece...the one that makes it whole...is missing." His shoulders slumped. "I'm not saying it right."

Eve thought he was saying it exactly right, because she had felt this way herself...many times. And if Matthew had been adopted by another family—one where she would not have had access to him—she would have felt it even more strongly.

Mary Ann's eyes filled with tears, and her lower lip trembled. "I—I thought you were happy."

"Mom," Matthew said. His eyes implored her to understand. "Of course I'm happy. Being happy has nothing to do with this."

Her tears spilled over.

"You've upset your mother, son," Tony said. He reached for the box of tissues sitting on the buffet nearby and handed Mary Ann one. He did not look at Eve.

"Mary Ann," Lucia said. "It's okay. Matthew didn't mean it. Did you, Matthew?" She didn't look at Eve, either, but then, she didn't know the truth of Matthew's background.

Eve said nothing. She was afraid to say anything, because for the past few minutes, an alien emotion had replaced her initial shock—hope. For the first time in eighteen years, she finally admitted to herself that she had always hoped that someday Matthew would know the truth. That someday she could openly declare him her son. That someday he would look at her and instead of calling her Aunt Eve, he would call her Mom.

Matthew sighed. His gaze met Eve's. *I'm sorry,* it seemed to say. *I know you understand, but I can see they don't.* Then he shrugged. "No, Gran, I didn't really mean I was going to do anything. I—I just wondered how you all would feel if I did a little investigating."

"I don't think it's a good idea," Tony said.

Long moments went by in uneasy silence. Everyone looked at their empty cups. The grandfather clock in the corner chimed the hour, and Ben, Tony's faithful yellow Lab, stirred restlessly under the table.

Finally Tony spoke. "Son, I think this is something that's better left alone."

Matthew looked as if he wanted to say something else, but Tony spoke again.

"Now apologize to your mother for upsetting her."

"I'm sorry, Mom." Matthew put his arm around Mary Ann and patted her head. "I didn't mean to hurt your feelings."

Tony nodded. He still avoided Eve's eyes. "Good. I'm glad that's settled."

Eve arrived at the office early Monday morning. As usual, when she'd been gone a few days, the messages were piled sky-high. In addition, two of her designers had crises that only she could solve, and her longtime bookkeeper had given her notice.

Eve prioritized, then one by one, she dealt with each message, each problem.

At ten o'clock, she presided over the regular Monday staff meeting, and it was during this meeting that the violets were delivered.

Eve tried to hide her pleasure when Tammi, the receptionist, brought in the squat lavender vase filled with the delicate blooms.

"Aren't you going to open the card?" Chloe said slyly as Eve turned her attention back to the meeting.

"Later," Eve said casually, ignoring the raised eyebrows and curious looks.

"New man in your life?" asked Keneesha, a designer who'd been with Eve since the inception of the company.

The staff continued to tease her until Eve threw up her hands and said, "Okay! Enough. Yes, I'm seeing someone new. And no, I'm not going to tell you his name. Now, can we please get back to discussing our Flower Garden collection?"

When the meeting was finally over, Eve escaped to the privacy of her office and once the door was closed from prying eyes, buried her face in the violets and breathed deeply. Then she opened the card.

I miss you so much, it hurts. All my love, Mitch.

Eve's eyes unexpectedly filled. She walked to the window and gazed out at the city spread beneath her. Oh, God, she missed him, too. Somehow, they simply had to work things out so they could be together. Too many years had already been wasted. She did not want to waste even an hour more. She squared her shoulders. And after tomorrow, when she would find a way to convince Mary Ann of what must be done, she wouldn't. Once that obstacle was taken care of, and Eve was free to be completely honest with Mitch, they could put the past behind them forever and go forward into the future.

Eve called at noon. "I got the flowers," she said. "They're so beautiful. Thank you."

Mitch closed his eyes. "God, it's so good to hear your voice. I feel like we've been apart for weeks instead of just hours."

"I know. I feel the same way."

They were both silent for a few seconds, then Mitch said, "I love you."

There was a little catch in her voice as she replied. "I love you, too."

"I can't wait until we can be together again."

"I know. Me, too."

"Last night, I couldn't fall asleep. It didn't seem right, being in bed without you."

He could almost hear her smile as she said, "No wonder, you're such a sex fiend."

He laughed. "The reason is, I went so long without any, now I have to make up for it."

Her voice turned serious again. "Really? You mean you haven't, uh, had a relationship since Carolyn died?"

He laughed again, pleased that she was uncomfortable asking him and doubly pleased that she felt possessive enough to want to know. "Nope. Not a one."

Now he was sure she was smiling.

"Know why?" he said.

"Too lazy?" she said lightly.

"No. It's because I compared everyone else to you. And they always came up short."

After they hung up, Mitch thought about their conversation. It was true what he'd told Eve—no one had ever compared to her. Unfortunately, it was not only true of after Carolyn died, it had also been true while he'd been married to her.

And she had known it.

He would never forget the night she had thrown the knowledge in his face.

May, ten years earlier

Mitch wanted to go home. He felt bone tired from a long week at work. But Carolyn had insisted on attending a party at the country club being thrown by Jack and Nadine Ingram for their seventh wedding anniversary. She had pouted and put on her injured act when he'd suggested she attend without him, and he'd finally given in.

Mitch didn't like the Ingrams. He thought Jack was crude and Nadine was mean spirited, but Jack's father owned the ceramics factory and Nadine's father was superintendent of the school board, which was all that mattered to Carolyn.

By eleven o'clock, Mitch thought if he heard one more joke and wink-wink about "the seven-year itch," he would puke. Finally, at twelve-thirty, when he'd reminded Carolyn that Betsy, their baby-sitter, had to be home by one, his wife consented to leave.

She gave him the cold shoulder on the way home. Mitch sighed. He never seemed able to please her. He had no idea what was eating her now, and what's more, he didn't care.

They arrived home, paid Betsy, and Mitch took the teenager home. And even though he couldn't wait to go to bed, when he got back to the house, he headed for the kitchen and poured himself a glass of milk. He knew it was cowardly, but he was putting off the moment when he'd have to join Carolyn, because no matter how angry she might be, it was Friday night, and he knew she would want sex. She used sex as a weapon, but rather than withholding it, as some women might do, she seemed to take great pleasure in demanding it, especially when they'd had some kind of earlier disagreement. Unfortunately for Mitch, those times seemed to come more and more frequently lately.

After drinking the milk, he rinsed his glass and carefully placed it in the dishwasher. Then he walked around downstairs, checked all the doors and windows, finally climbing the stairs to the second level.

He tiptoed into Nicholas's room first. His son lay curled up hugging a bedraggled teddy bear. His covers had been kicked off. Mitch swallowed around the lump of love that snagged in his throat. His feelings for his five-year-old son were so intense they sometimes scared him.

No matter how bad things got between Mitch and Carolyn, Mitch knew that he would never leave her, because he could never leave Nicholas. And Carolyn knew that. She knew it, and she used her knowledge like a club to keep Mitch in line.

He smoothed a lock of hair from Nicholas's face, bent over the sleeping child and kissed his warm cheek. "Sleep tight, sport," he whispered. "I love you."

Nicholas stirred, but he didn't wake.

Mitch gently pulled up the cotton comforter and tucked it around Nicholas, then quietly headed for his own bedroom.

The room was dim, lit only by a crack of light coming from the bathroom.

Mitch looked at the bed. Carolyn was turned away from him, but he knew she was still awake. He quietly entered the bathroom, dawdling through his nighttime rituals.

When he finally slipped into the bed, he turned on his side, facing away from her. He closed his eyes.

Minutes passed, then he felt her turn. He stiffened involuntarily when her lips touched his back and her hand crept around his waist to loosen the drawstring on his pajama bottoms.

"I'm exhausted, Carolyn," he said.

For a long moment she lay still. Then she removed her hand, and a second later, she snapped on her bedside lamp.

He sighed. "What are you doing?"

"If you're so exhausted," she said tightly, "then I have to do *something* to relax me. I'm going to read." She plumped up her pillow and sat up defiantly.

Mitch bit back the words he wanted to say. He shrugged. "Okay." He rolled back on his side and resolutely closed his yes.

A minute later, she said, "You don't care at all, do you?"

Oh, please, Carolyn, not tonight. As much as he would have liked to ignore her, he knew from past experience that she would not be denied. "What do you mean?"

"Will you please turn around and *look* at me when I'm talking to you?"

Sighing, he sat up.

"I mean, you don't care about our marriage and you don't care about me."

"That's ridiculous, and you know it." *He had spent the past ten years trying to make a go of his marriage.*

"Oh, now I'm ridiculous."

"Carolyn, please, I've had a long day...can't we discuss this some other time?"

Angry tears shone in her eyes. "You hate me, don't you?"

"I don't hate you. I'm just tired—"

"You've always hated me. You didn't want to marry me, and you've never let me forget it."

He stared at her. So she wanted to play hardball tonight. Well, two could play this game. "After I found out you'd lied to me about being pregnant, I was angry. But I haven't said a word to you about the circumstances of our marriage since then. And you know it."

"You didn't have to say it. I knew what you were thinking."

"It's your own guilty conscience at work that makes you feel that way."

"Oh, naturally, everything is my fault. Everything is always my fault."

He sighed again. "Carolyn, there's no point to this."

"It's *her,* isn't it? You're still in love with *her!*"

Mitch had never told Carolyn Eve's name, thank God, because there was no telling what she would do if she had any idea his youthful love had become someone so successful and famous. She was eaten alive with jealousy now. Knowing Eve's identity would have made Mitch's life even more intolerable than it had become.

"Who is she?" Carolyn shouted. "Tell me who she is! I think I have a right to know my rival."

"Keep your voice down," he said. "You'll wake Nicholas."

"I don't care!" She started to cry, great hiccuping sobs.

Mitch was suddenly òverwhelmed by pity. Carolyn wasn't a bad person. She was spoiled, but she was also frightened and vulnerable. He knew that. He also knew, in her twisted way, she really loved him, and she was scared to death that she would eventually lose him.

He reached for her, smoothing her hair and patting her back and saying comforting things. And when she finally calmed down and raised a tear-streaked face to his, he voiced no further objections.

"Here you are!" Chloe said, walking into the little kitchenette that served as a lunchroom for Eve's staff, at eleven o'clock on Tuesday morning. "I've been looking all over for you. Two things. Kenny wants to know what you think about this material for the Rose model?" Chloe handed Eve a swatch of rose crepe. "And your sister-in-law's on line two."

Eve finished stirring lemon in her tea. "Leave the swatch and tell Kenny I'll get back to him." She reached for the wall phone, punched the button for line two and said, "Hi, Mary Ann. Are you at the apartment?"

"Yes. I just got in."

"Have a good trip down?" Eve held the swatch up to the light. Nice tight weave, she thought.

"It was okay. The train wasn't too crowded."

Not for the first time, Eve realized how all of Mary Ann's sentences were negative. Had her sister-in-law always been this way? Or was her negativity simply a result of her loneliness after first her mother's, then Tony's death? "Well," Eve said brightly, "why don't you get unpacked and have some lunch? Before Margaret left yesterday, she made crab salad, and it's in the refrigerator. And there are fresh strawberries and some of those rolls you like from Balducci's."

"All right. When will you be home?"

"I'll leave the office early and be home by four," Eve promised.

It was actually four-fifteen before Eve entered the Fifth Avenue building that housed her apartment. "Hello, Harold," she said to the doorman.

"Afternoon, Miss DelVecchio," he said, tipping his hat.

Eve waved to the security guard, then headed for the elevators. As she rode up to the fifteenth floor, she decided she would not talk to Mary Ann about Mitch and Matthew today. Tomorrow or Thursday was soon enough. In the meantime, she would try to get Mary Ann in a better frame of mind. *Soften her up, you mean.* She winced. That sounded so calculated.

The elevator doors slid open and she walked out into the entry hall leading to her apartment. She unlocked the front door and stepped inside a square foyer. To the right, an archway led into her spacious living room.

As always, Eve felt a quiet pleasure when she entered the living room. Furnished in a blend of deep-cushioned contemporary furniture in shades of taupe, navy and dusty rose and graceful antique accent pieces, it never failed to soothe her. It was large enough to hold fifty people comfortably for a cocktail party, and at least a dozen for a smaller, more intimate evening. At the moment, the room was flooded with afternoon sunshine but was otherwise empty.

Eve circled through the apartment, looking for Mary Ann. The large blue-tiled kitchen was also empty. Before leaving the kitchen, Eve glanced in the refrigerator. She was pleased to see that Mary Ann had eaten some of the crab salad. Her sister-in-law couldn't afford to lose any more weight.

Eve headed into the bedroom wing. After depositing her purse and briefcase in her office, which adjoined her bedroom, she walked down the hall and knocked softly on the guest room door.

"Umph?" came the muffled reply.

Eve opened the door. The heavy drapes on the windows facing East Eighty-First Street had been drawn, and the room was dim. "Mary Ann?" she said softly. "You awake?"

A sound that was a cross between a sigh and a yawn was her answer, then Mary Ann snapped on the bedside light.

Eve walked over to the bed and sat on the side. She looked at the woman who was struggling to sit up.

Mary Ann looked like hell. Her hair, which had always been thick and dark, was heavily gray. That would be fine, because the gray was actually very attractive, but Mary Ann had let herself go in the past year, and her hair was no exception. It was too long and too straight for her narrow face. Her makeup, if she'd worn any earlier, had worn off, including her lipstick, so her face looked wan and pale. Her dark brown eyes, always one of her best features, were clouded and dull.

And her clothes! Eve resisted the urge to grab Mary Ann and shake her. Those brown slacks and white blouse were the most unattractive clothes Eve had ever seen.

Eve told herself to be understanding, so all she said was, "Have a good nap?"

Mary Ann nodded and made a halfhearted attempt at a smile. "What time is it?"

"Almost four-thirty."

"Guess I'd better get up."

Eve stood. "Come on into my bedroom while I change into something more comfortable. I thought we'd just eat in tonight, if that's all right with you."

"Sure. That's fine." Mary Ann's expression altered almost imperceptibly. "We have something important to talk about anyway."

Eve frowned, wondering what was on Mary Ann's mind as she led the way into her bedroom. She waved her sister-in-law to the silk brocade love seat in the corner, then opened the doors to the walk-in closet and began unbuttoning her cocoa linen dress.

When Mary Ann said nothing, Eve spoke up. "What is it you wanted to talk about?"

"It's Matthew."

Alarm skidded through Eve, but just as quickly receded. If something had happened to him, Mary Ann would be hysterical.

"Have you talked to him since you got back?" Mary Ann asked.

"Yes, I called him last night." Eve turned to hang up her dress.

"Did he mention anything about . . . wanting to find his birth parents again?"

Eve was glad her back was turned to Mary Ann. "No. Why? Has he brought it up again?" She removed her pumps and placed them in their see-through plastic box before slowly turning to face Mary Ann again.

Mary Ann's eyes showed their first real animation since Eve's arrival. "Yes. And he seems really determined this time. I won't have it, Eve. You've got to talk him out of it. You've got to. Do you understand?"

Eve reached for her favorite at-home outfit, a black silk caftan. She slipped it on before answering. "But Mary Ann, we can't really stop him from investigating, you know. And, anyway, don't you think it's time—"

"No!" Mary Ann jumped up. She glared at Eve. "No. I do *not* think it's time to tell him, and as long as I live, I never will." Her eyes looked like two fiery, dark coals burning in her pinched, unhappy face. "I've lost too much. I do not intend to lose Matthew, too."

Chapter Fourteen

Eve told herself to stay calm as she walked out of the closet, her bare feet sinking into the thick white carpeting.

Mary Ann stood, defiance written into every part of her body language.

Eve kept her voice quiet and calm, just as if her entire future were not at stake here. "Now don't get upset, Mary Ann. Listen, let's go out to the living room and I'll pour us some wine, and we can sit and talk about this in comfort."

"Fine, we can go sit down, but I have no intention of discussing this subject anymore."

Eve used the time it took to reach the living room and pour them each a glass of chardonnay to marshal her wits and soothe her frazzled nerves. When she felt ready to face her sister-in-law again, she carried the wineglasses over to the couch and handed Mary Ann one.

Then she sat at the opposite end of the sofa and propped her bare feet on the coffee table. She took a sip of her wine. Only then did she look at Mary Ann.

Mary's Ann return gaze was antagonistic, as if she knew Eve had no intention of dropping the subject of Matthew's parentage.

Please, God, help me do this the right way. "I wasn't going to mention this tonight, but since you've brought up the subject, I—I have something to tell you, too. Something that might make a difference in how you feel."

"Nothing's going to make a difference."

"Please. Just hear me out, okay?" When Mary Ann didn't object, Eve continued. "Something happened while I was in Ohio. Something really wonderful."

Mary Ann sat silently, her face stony.

Eve swallowed. Mary Ann wasn't going to make it easier for her. "I—I saw Matthew's father again."

Mary Ann's eyes widened in shock and she opened her mouth as if to speak.

Before her sister-in-law could say anything, Eve hurriedly added, "He's a widower now, and we spent quite a bit of time together." She took a deep breath. "We . . . we discovered we still love each other, and he's asked me to marry him."

Mary Ann stared at Eve.

"I know you'll agree that I can't marry him without telling him about Matthew. So I'm asking you to release me from my promise. It's only a matter of time, anyway, because obviously Matthew isn't going to drop the sub—"

"If you think I'm going to give you my blessing, you're crazy." Mary Ann set her wineglass on the coffee table so hard Eve winced. Then she stood, her face flooded with anger and resentment and something else. Something wild and frightening.

"Please, Mary Ann, sit down. Don't get so upset. If we could just talk quietly, if you'd just listen for a—"

"No! I won't listen to you. I want you to listen to me for a change." She sneered. "You make me sick, do you know that? You've had it so easy your entire life. Everyone has petted you and spoiled you and smoothed your way, acting as if the sun rose and set on your head. Especially Tony. All of my married life I had to listen to how wonderful you were—how smart, how pretty, how clever." She took a ragged breath. "Tony placed you on a pedestal. He thought you were perfect. And then you got pregnant. By a married man, no less. But did that disillusion Tony? Oh, no. Of course not. Because even there you managed to best me." Her face twisted. "You gave him the son I couldn't give him." Angry tears flooded her eyes.

Eve felt as if Mary Ann were throwing knives at her. She had known Mary Ann resented her close relationship with Matthew, but she'd had no idea her sister-in-law had harbored such deep and bitter feelings for so long.

"You've had everything! You didn't even suffer because of your illegitimate pregnancy. You had someone to raise your child, you could see him whenever you wanted to, and you were free to pursue your career. To get rich and famous. And now," Mary Ann said, the tears finally erupting, "now that it's *convenient* for you, you want Matthew back. Well, you can't have him! I won't let you take him! He's *my* son. I'm the one who sat up with him at night when he was sick. I'm the one who went to all the PTO meetings, who baked the brownies, who drove on the field trips. You're the one who traveled all over the world without a care. Well, you can talk until you're blue in the face, but I'll *never* release you from your promise!''

"Mary Ann," Eve said, trying to hold back her own hurt and pain, "I don't want to take Matthew away from you, but even if I did, I couldn't. Just because he knew the circumstances of his birth wouldn't change things. He'd still be your son. I—I don't want to take your place."

"Ha! That's funny, you know that? You've been trying to take my place in Matthew's affections from the very beginning, and don't think I haven't known it!"

"That's not true! I never did—"

"You *always* did! Buying him everything we could never afford to give him. His car. His fancy education. Even the house we live in! Making him think you were some kind of fairy godmother or something. Oh, I know what you've been doing. I'm not stupid." She swiped at her tears. "You're selfish, Eve. You always have been. Everything is always you, you, you. As long as you get *your* way, you don't care how many lives you ruin, do you?"

"I—I never knew you felt this way," Eve whispered.

"I'm warning you, Eve! If you say anything... anything at all..." Her voice rose hysterically. "I won't be responsible for what I do!" Then she swung around and raced out of the room.

Feeling completely battered by the force of Mary Ann's hostility, Eve sat there for long minutes and tried to think what she should do. Part of her wanted to go after Mary Ann and say hurtful things to her, too. But the other part, the compassionate, understanding, mature part of her knew she couldn't do that. Mary Ann was obviously terrified. She was also insecure and lonely and depressed, perhaps even clinically depressed. Tonight's episode had shown Eve just how close to the edge Mary Ann really was. Eve couldn't do anything to push her over that edge—not and live with herself.

She waited until she felt calmer, then rose and headed for the guest room. The door stood open, and Mary Ann was throwing her clothes into her suitcase.

Dear God, how did things deteriorate to this point? "Mary Ann, please. Don't leave."

Mary Ann ignored her, tossing the last garment into the suitcase and slamming it shut. When she turned around, her face looked ravaged. "Would you please call me a cab?" she said tightly.

Eve could see how her sister-in-law was struggling to maintain control. Eve had never felt so helpless. She knew it would be hopeless to try to change Mary Ann's mind while she was in this state. "I don't want you taking the train home at night. I'll call Leo. He'll drive you," she said calmly. Eve kept a car in a nearby garage, and Leo was a driver she used occasionally.

"Fine."

Eve didn't know what else to say. She felt completely drained by Mary Ann's attack. She didn't dare think about what all of this meant. Time enough for that when Mary Ann was gone. "I'll go call him now."

Eve escaped into her office. Just as she finished punching in Leo's number, she heard Mary Ann walk past the open door. She hurriedly gave the driver her instructions, then called downstairs to let the guard know Leo was coming. When she was finished, she headed for the living room again.

Mary Ann stood looking out the window. Her back was to Eve, and she didn't turn when Eve entered the room.

"Leo will be here in about thirty minutes," Eve said.
"Okay."

Eve stood there indecisively. After a few seconds, she said, "Would you like another glass of wine while you're waiting? Or something to eat? It's going to be late when you get home."

"No." Mary Ann looked around. "You don't have to wait here with me. I'm perfectly all right alone. After all, I'm used to it."

Their gazes met. Eve suppressed the desire to shiver. How could she have gone all these years without knowing how Mary Ann really felt about her?

"Mary Ann," Eve said softly. "I feel awful about all of this. I don't want us to part this way. If only for Matthew's sake, we've got to find a way to get past this."

Mary Ann looked away, but a muscle in her jaw twitched.

"We both said things we didn't really mean..." Eve began, determined to put pride out of the way, to say whatever it took to achieve at least a semblance of normalcy between them.

"Speak for yourself. I meant every word I said," was Mary Ann's tight-lipped reply.

Eve threw up her hands. "Oh, for heaven's sake! I was just trying to give you a face-saving out, but you don't want one, do you? You're *glad* you said all those things. You wish I'd just disappear from your life, don't you?" When her sister-in-law didn't answer, Eve said, "All right. Have it your way. Wait by yourself." She whipped around, even started to walk away, but something in her had to make one last try. "I'll be in my office if you need me."

"I won't."

Twenty-five minutes later, the doorbell rang and Mary Ann left. She didn't say goodbye.

Three days had passed since Mary Ann's abrupt departure, and Eve had not heard from her. Several times, she had been tempted to call her sister-in-law, but she changed her mind at the last minute. What could she say?

Eve didn't know what to do. She'd gone over and over her options. Ignoring Mary Ann and telling both Mitch and Matthew the truth was one of them, but she'd already discarded it. She just couldn't take the chance that she might cause Mary Ann to do something crazy. And Matthew had to be a consideration, too. What would he think of Eve if she caused his mother such unhappiness?

Besides, she made a deal all those years ago. Mary Ann had lived up to her end. So no matter how unreasonable she might seem now, or how hard it was on Eve, she had to continue to live up to her end until Mary Ann said it was all right not to.

The second option was to marry Mitch and not tell him about Matthew. The success of this option was based on two assumptions. The first was that Nicholas would accept her. And the second was that she could actually keep such a secret from Mitch. Right now she wasn't sure of either, especially her ability to hide something so fundamental.

Her final option was to break off with Mitch. The thought of doing so made her feel sick.

Face it. You're in a no-win situation.

Suddenly she just had to hear Mitch's voice. She looked at the clock. It was a little after nine. Mitch had said Nicholas's flight would arrive at noon. She picked up the phone and pressed the numbers for Mitch's office.

"Eve!" he said. "This is a nice surprise. I didn't expect to hear from you this morning."

As always, his voice had the effect of soothing balm on her aching spirit. "Hi." She picked up a crystal apple paperweight, closing her palm around its solid weight. "I was thinking about you, and I just had an irresistible urge to call."

His voice lowered. "I'm glad you did."

"I miss you," she said around the lump in her throat.

"Not half as much as I miss you."

"I'm not sure I can wait another week to see you."

"Then don't," he said. "I wanted you to come earlier than Friday, anyway. Just give me a day or so with Nicholas first, then come."

She wanted to. She knew it was absurd, but she had the feeling that if only she could be with Mitch, everything would be all right. As if, somehow, their problems would disappear. "I wish I could, but I think it's better if we just stick to our plan." Maybe, by some miracle, Mary Ann would see reason and call Eve before Friday. *Oh, sure, and pigs fly, don't they?*

"You sound kind of down. Is something wrong?"

"Oh, no," she said quickly. "I told you. I just miss you." She made her voice determinedly cheerful. "Are you excited about seeing Nicholas?"

"Yeah, I am. It'll be good to have him back."

"What time are you leaving for the airport?"

"About eleven, I guess."

"Will you go back to the office afterward?"

"No, I'm going to take the rest of the day off. I figured we'd go home, get him unpacked, then I'm sure he's going to want to call his friends. Especially Shannon Flynn.'' Mitch chuckled. ''I hope he didn't miss her as much as I miss you.''

''I didn't know he had a girlfriend.''

''Yeah, well, they've been pretty inseparable the past year. I worried about it for a while. The emotions of teenagers can get pretty intense, and they really don't have the maturity or judgment to go along with them.''

Tell me about it. ''Yes, that's true.''

''I sound overprotective, don't I?''

''No. Just sensible.''

They were both silent for a while, lost in their own thoughts. Then he said softly, ''You know what I wish?''

''What?''

''I wish Nicholas was our son. Yours and mine. I've always wished that. Sometimes at night, when I'd go in his room to kiss him good-night, I'd pretend he was. I'd pretend that when I left him and went into the bedroom, you'd be there.'' He made a funny, self-deprecating sound. ''You probably think I'm nuts, but I would have given anything to have you be the mother of my son.''

Eve could feel the tears forming in the backs of her eyes. *Oh, Mitch, I'm so sorry. So very sorry.* ''That's the sweetest thing anyone's ever said to me,'' she said softly.

''I love you, Eve,'' he murmured. ''Hurry back, will you? I've spent too much time without you already. I don't want to spend any more time apart.''

Mitch got to the airport early. He couldn't wait to see Nicholas. A month was a long time.

The flight came in on time. Even so, Mitch waited impatiently at the entrance to the jetway. He grinned when he saw the familiar head of hair.

"Dad!" Nicholas waved and grinned.

Mitch gave him a bear hug, then they slapped each other on the back and laughed. "Where're your grand-parents?" Mitch said.

"They're coming."

A minute later Joanna and Charles Whittaker emerged from the jetway and cordial greetings were ex-changed all around. For a fleeting moment, Mitch wondered how happy they'd be to see him if they had any idea what had happened to him in the past couple of weeks.

It was a sobering thought. He knew they would not be overjoyed to have him remarry. They would view a second marriage as a betrayal of their daughter's mem-ory. Well, they'd just have to get over any negative feelings, because no one was going to keep him from being with Eve. The Whittakers would come around eventually, he figured. They wouldn't want to do any-thing to jeopardize their relationship with Nicholas.

Despite Mitch's certainty of this eventuality, he was grateful that they had never known about Eve. He was sure Carolyn had never confided in them. She would have been too embarrassed to admit that he hadn't wanted to marry her. Good thing, too, because it would be impossible for Mitch to maintain a cordial relation-ship with them if they did know. They would not be able to hide their resentment, which would make his and Eve's life together much more difficult than it needed to be. As it was, he knew they had always been per-plexed about why Carolyn had been so unhappy in the last few years before her death. But being the kind of people they were, they had never voiced their questions, and Mitch had never volunteered any information.

"It's good to be home," Charles said as they headed off toward the baggage pickup. Because the travelers had so much luggage, they would travel back to Maple Hills in two vehicles—Mitch's car and a cab.

"I'll ride in the cab," Charles said. "You ride with Mitch and Nicholas, Joanna."

Joanna, a petite blonde like her daughter had been, didn't object.

Soon they were on their way. Nicholas talked nonstop all the way home, with his grandmother interjecting a comment here and there—mostly to correct perceived inaccuracies or exaggerations in his stories.

"And then, Dad, we knew we were lost, but Granddad refused to stop and ask for directions!" Nicholas said gleefully.

"Typical man," Joanna said.

Mitch laughed. "So what happened?"

"Well, we drove and drove, and Gran kept saying, 'We're lost, Charles, why won't you admit it?' and Granddad kept saying, 'I know exactly where we are!'" Nicholas mimicked both grandparents perfectly.

"I knew exactly where we were, too," Joanna said, voice dripping with sarcasm, "because we'd passed the same statue at least five times. We'd been going around in a perfect circle for more than forty-five minutes. Honestly, as long as I live, I'll *never* understand men."

Mitch winked at Nicholas, and Nicholas grinned.

They reached the Whittakers' house at one-thirty. By the time they'd unloaded the older couple's luggage, carried it all into the house, said their goodbyes and started for home, it was after two.

"You hungry, sport?" Mitch said. "Want to stop and have some pizza?"

"At Albertini's?" Nicholas said, naming his favorite pizza place.

"Where else?"

By two-thirty, they were settled into a booth in the small restaurant, tall mugs of root beer in front of them. Nicholas had finally wound down, and Mitch decided this was as good a time as ever to tell him about Eve.

"You know how you've been encouraging me to date?" he said.

Nicholas's blue eyes, the only physical characteristic he'd inherited from his mother, twinkled. "Hey," he teased, "you mean you actually got up the old nerve and asked somebody to go out with you?"

Mitch smiled.

"Who is she? Anybody I know?"

"Remember when I told you I was going to that reception at the country club? The one honoring that famous designer who used to live in Maple Hills?"

"Yeah."

"Well, she's the one."

Nicholas grinned. "Famous, huh? What's her name?"

"Eve DelVecchio."

"I never heard of her."

"Her design label is Eden."

"Oh. Yeah, I've heard of that."

Just then their name was called, and Nicholas went to pick up their pizza. When he got back, they each took a slice. Mitch waited a few seconds, then said, "How would you feel about me getting married again?"

Nicholas's eyes widened. "Married again? Man, you're a fast worker!"

Mitch smiled. "Not that fast. I, uh, used to know Eve when I was young."

"Really? Before you and Mom got together?"

"Something like that."

Nicholas took a huge bite of pizza, cheese stringing out and trailing down his chin.

Mitch watched him, thinking how much Nicholas meant to him. Thinking how much he wanted Nicholas to love Eve. Thinking how much he wanted the three of them to be a family. "Well?" he said after a few moments. "What do you think?"

"I don't know, Dad. I gotta think about it awhile." Nicholas drank about a third of his root beer, then reached for another slice of pizza.

"I know this is kind of sudden, but I really care for Eve, and I hope you will, too."

"When am I gonna meet her?" Nicholas said around another enormous bite.

Mitch ate some of his pizza, too. "She's coming back to Maple Hills on Friday."

Nicholas nodded.

"I thought we could have dinner together that night, and maybe on Saturday we could all go to Kings Island. You could invite Shannon to go, too."

Nicholas grinned. "A double date, huh?"

Mitch grinned, too. He felt good about this. He felt good about everything. Even though Nicholas hadn't shown unqualified enthusiasm over the possibility of Mitch's remarrying, he hadn't seemed against the idea. He'd come around. Mitch was sure of it. When he met Eve, he would fall under her spell, just as Mitch had.

And when that happened, Eve would no longer have any doubts about their future together.

How could she?

All their troubles would be behind them.

Eve arrived back in Maple Hills at four o'clock the following Friday. She had spoken with Mitch the previous evening, and they'd arranged for him to come by the inn to pick her up at six. They were having dinner with Nicholas at Mitch's house.

Eve tried to empty her mind of everything but how happy she would be to see Mitch again.

She dressed carefully. She wanted to make a good impression on Nicholas. Mitch had said it would be a casual evening, so she'd brought a pair of royal blue gabardine slacks and matching summer-weight sweater. With it she wore chunky silver jewelry and a pair of soft blue leather flats.

She took pains with her hair, leaving it soft and loose around her face. She wanted to leave her sophisticated, New York, successful persona behind. Tonight she just wanted to be Eve, born and raised in Maple Hills. Someone Nicholas could feel comfortable with.

Nicholas.

Her emotions were so mixed. She wanted him to like her. And she wanted to like him.

Yet there was another part of her that couldn't help feeling a vague resentment. Nicholas was not just Mitch's son. He was Carolyn's son. If not for Carolyn, Matthew would be the son Mitch adored.

Oh, God, her feelings were so crazy! She knew she would have to get over any negative ones if she hoped to build any kind of future with Mitch.

And she would.

She kept telling herself everything would work out. It had to work out. She wouldn't, she *couldn't*, live without Mitch again.

As the minutes passed, Eve grew increasingly nervous. Tonight was so important. Tonight held the key to whether there was any hope for her and Mitch.

Finally six o'clock came. Mitch said he'd come up to her suite—the same one she'd occupied before. She knew why he didn't want to meet in the lobby. He didn't want alien eyes watching their meeting. Neither did she.

His knock on the door came at one minute after six. Pressing her hands against her stomach to still the butterflies, Eve walked to the door and opened it.

Without words, he took her in his arms. His kiss told her how much he'd missed her, how much he wanted her, how much he loved her.

Afterward he held her close. She closed her eyes, feeling the warmth and solid comfort of his body. "Don't ever leave me again," he whispered against her hair.

She smiled and raised her face.

They gazed into each other's eyes.

"I love you," he said.

"I love you."

He kissed her mouth softly. "Ready?"

"Ready."

As they drove to his house, she couldn't stop looking at him. She thought about what he'd said at the hotel. *Don't ever leave me again.* She didn't want to. If only she could be absolutely sure she would be able to live with the burden of her secret. What if it proved intolerable? What if it slowly eroded their relationship?

Please, God, she prayed. *Let this work out for us. Give me some sign that what I'm contemplating doing is the best thing. Show me that it'll be all right.*

At six-twenty, they pulled into Mitch's driveway. The butterflies started up again. Mitch cut the ignition and turned to her. He smiled. "You're not nervous, are you?"

"No," she lied.

They got out of the car. Walked up the back steps. Through the screened-in porch. The inner door stood open. Mitch waved her ahead of him.

Taking a deep breath, Eve walked into the kitchen.

She heard footsteps racing down the stairs, heading toward them.

Her heartbeat accelerated.

Mitch grinned. He put his arm around her shoulders, holding her close to his side. "Here comes Nicholas," he said, giving her an encouraging squeeze.

A boy appeared in the doorway a second later. He smiled. "Hi!"

All Eve could do was stare in stunned and horrified disbelief.

The teenager who stood before her was the spitting image of Matthew, right down to the shock of white hair that grew just to the right of the middle of his forehead.

Chapter Fifteen

Everything about Nicholas—his height, his body shape, his square jaw, the shape of his eyes, his smile—were identical to his half brother's. The only difference was the color of his hair and his eyes. Nicholas's hair was lighter, more brown than black, and his eyes were blue. Matthew's hair was as dark as Eve's, and his eyes were hazel, like Mitch's.

Eve stared, dumbfounded.

The differences were minor.

No one, seeing Nicholas and Matthew together, could ever mistake them for anything other than brothers.

No one who knew both boys could ever doubt their shared parentage.

Even if, by some miracle, Mary Ann could have been persuaded to allow Eve to tell only Mitch the truth, there was no way—now—that the secret could remain in their family.

As all these thoughts careened through her mind, Mitch was drawing her forward, saying, "Eve, this is my son, Nicholas. Nicholas, I'd like you to meet Eve— Eve DelVecchio."

"Hi, Miss DelVecchio," Nicholas said. "It's nice to meet you."

Eve tried to smile. She tried to act as if she hadn't just been given the shock of her life. She knew her attempt was pitiful, because she was still reeling from the ramifications of her discovery, and it was nearly impossible to disguise the chaos going on inside her. She finally managed to say a shaky, "H-hello, Nicholas."

Nicholas's smile faltered, and he looked at his father. His expression said, *what's going on here?*

"Eve?" Mitch said. "Is something wrong?"

Eve rallied enough to stammer, "Wrong? N-no, I, uh, guess I'm more nervous than I thought." She couldn't stop staring at Nicholas.

Mitch chuckled. "Nicholas won't bite."

Eve struggled to pull herself together. "Your father tells me you really enjoyed your first trip to Europe." Her voice sounded almost normal, but inside, she ached with the knowledge that she could never hope to keep Matthew's real identity a secret from Mitch. The moment he met her so-called nephew, he would know the truth.

Nicholas launched into an enthusiastic answer, and Eve used the time to further compose herself. She must not let Mitch see that she was upset. She did not want him asking questions. Not now, anyway. She had to have some time to think.

Somehow she managed to get through the evening. Somehow she laughed and talked and ate. Somehow she pretended everything was great. But sitting across the table from Nicholas was one of the hardest things she'd ever had to do.

He was everything his father had said he was: polite, nice, an all-around terrific kid. Under any other circumstances, she would be thrilled with him. And he seemed to really like her, too—that was the kicker. He seemed genuinely happy for his father, and Eve knew that if she did marry Mitch, Nicholas would not present a problem.

If she did marry Mitch...

What was she thinking of?

She couldn't marry Mitch.

And no amount of wishing was going to change that irrefutable fact.

But how on earth was she going to break off with him? Not only would it tear her apart inside, but what kind of reason could she give?

She certainly couldn't use Nicholas as an excuse. If he'd been rude to her or if he'd treated her with hostility or resentment, maybe then she'd have a logical reason...but he hadn't. No youngster could be more mannerly or warmly welcoming than Nicholas.

On and on her thoughts marched, as outwardly she put on the greatest acting job of her life.

Finally the evening was over.

Finally it was time for Mitch to take her back to the hotel.

"Don't wait up for me, sport," Mitch said. "I, uh, might be awhile."

Nicholas grinned. "Don't be too late."

They both laughed, and Eve knew Mitch must have said those identical words many times.

"Good night, Nicholas," Eve said. "I really enjoyed meeting you. Y-you're every bit as great as your father said you were." The words cost her dearly—she already had a lump in her throat—but Nicholas deserved them.

Nicholas flushed with pleasure. "You are, too," he said hurriedly, ducking his head and evidencing his first bout of shyness. "See you tomorrow," he added as they walked out the door.

"See?" Mitch said once they were out of earshot of Nicholas. "You were worried for nothing. Didn't I tell you everything would be fine? I knew he'd be crazy about you." He pulled her close. "Everything's going to be great."

Eve couldn't answer. She kept her head averted and just nodded.

Luckily her silence didn't seem to bother Mitch.

The trip to the hotel took fifteen minutes, but to Eve, it seemed only a heartbeat before they were there.

And then another heartbeat before they stood outside the double doors of her suite. She fumbled in her purse for the key.

"Here, let me," Mitch said. He smiled down at her as he opened the door.

Eve knew the moment the doors closed behind them he would take her into his arms. She told herself she would have to be strong, stronger than she'd ever been before.

She knew she should tell him immediately. But she wanted this one last kiss. She needed this one last kiss. The memory of it would be something she could cherish in all the lonely years ahead.

She closed her eyes and let her purse slide to the floor as Mitch's hungry mouth claimed hers. She clung to him, pouring all of her desperation and sorrow into her response.

"I love you so much," he murmured as he finally ended the kiss. He nuzzled her temple. "We're going to be so happy—a real family." He cradled her close, stroking her hair. "And who knows? Maybe we'll even have a child of our own someday...a little brother or sister for Nicholas. Would you like that?"

Eve's eyes filled. "Mitch," she whispered brokenly, "I can't. I just can't marry you."

"What?" He laughed in disbelief. "Don't be silly. Of course, you can marry me. You're *going* to marry me, and the sooner, the better."

"No, no I can't." The cry was torn from her heart.

"What are you talking about?" His face was a picture of stunned incredulity.

"I—I realized tonight that it—it's never going to work," she stammered. Pain stabbed her chest, making it hard to breathe.

"Eve..." Mitch pulled back, lifting her chin so that he could look at her face. His eyes were puzzled. "You're not making sense. Tonight was perfect. Nicholas is nuts about you. I could tell."

"It—it's not Nicholas." *God, please help me. Please don't let me break down.*

"I don't understand." Mitch's expression, his entire body, radiated bewilderment.

"I—I'm sorry. I never meant to hurt you, but we—we're just so different. It would never work."

"What do you mean? That's crazy, Eve. You said it yourself, when we were in Saint James. We belong together. We've always belonged together."

Eve searched desperately for something she could say that would convince him. Something he would believe. "I used to think that, yes, especially when we were in Saint James, but Mitch, that was just...just the romantic atmosphere. Tonight . . . tonight I realized I was wrong. I could never be a part of your world."

He shook his head. "You don't mean that."

She knew she had to get it all out before she lost her nerve. "I do mean it. It would be a big mistake for us to marry. A very big mistake, because I wouldn't be happy here. I saw that tonight. And you just wouldn't fit in in New York." Her heart felt as if someone had opened it and was draining it of life. She knew she was hurting him just as much as she would be if she were sticking him with a knife, but what other choice did she have? Calling on her last bit of strength, she forced herself to laugh lightly. "Why, even the thought of living this provincial kind of life makes me shudder. And have a baby? If you knew me at all, you'd know I'm not the motherly type."

He stared at her. "But how could you . . ." He swallowed. "You said you loved me."

Oh, Mitch. I'm sorry. I'm so very, very sorry. This isn't fair. I know it's not fair. We both deserve better than this. She hadn't thought she had any strength left, but somehow she managed to shove the knife deeper. "I know. I guess I made the same mistake I made when we were kids. I mistook great sex and physical attraction for love."

He stiffened. "Great sex? That's it? That's all the past weeks have meant to you?"

She shrugged and laced her voice with amusement. "I know your pride is probably hurt, but yes . . . I'm afraid that's right." She winced at the hurt in his eyes—a hurt he managed to cover within seconds.

"I see," he said coldly. "In that case, I guess we have nothing more to say to each other, do we?"

A moment later he was gone.

* * *

Eve was sick. Sick at heart. Sick at body. For days she sat in her apartment, barely eating and barely sleeping. She refused to see or talk to anyone. She had Margaret, her housekeeper, tell all callers that she was ill and couldn't come to the phone.

Concerned friends sent flowers and plants and fruit. Chloe called every day.

Eve didn't care. She didn't talk to any of them, and she didn't care what they thought. She didn't care about anything.

She had never hurt like this. The hurt she'd felt as a seventeen-year-old was nothing compared to this agony, this total emptiness of spirit. She felt as if someone had taken her insides and removed them and left only this vacant shell that was her exterior.

She lost weight.

Dark circles appeared under her eyes.

"Miss DelVecchio," Margaret said on Thursday, nearly a week since Eve had last seen Mitch, "I think I should call the doctor." The older woman's gray eyes were the picture of concern.

Eve shook her head. "I don't need a doctor." *I just need Mitch, and no doctor can give him to me.*

"But Miss DelVecchio, something is *wrong,*" Margaret said.

"I said, no doctor."

"Well, do you want me to call Mr. Matthew or Mrs. DelVecchio?"

Eve started to laugh. Oh, that was funny. That was really, really funny. Matthew or Mary Ann. Oh, sure. Just what she needed. She could imagine the look of satisfaction on Mary Ann's face if she were to see how

Eve was suffering. She'd probably think Eve had gotten just what she deserved.

Margaret stared at her. Now her eyes were alarmed.

As quickly as she'd started, Eve stopped laughing. Her voice was curt as she said, "No, I do not want you to call Matthew or Mrs. DelVecchio. In fact, I want you to mind your own business." The minute the words were out of Eve's mouth, she was sorry, especially when she saw the injured look Margaret tried to hide.

"I apologize," Margaret said stiffly.

"Margaret, I'm sorry. I didn't mean that."

For the rest of the day, Margaret avoided Eve, and Eve didn't blame her.

On Friday, Matthew called. Eve told Margaret to tell him she couldn't come to the phone but she would call him back.

Hours later, when Eve had finally mustered enough courage to face talking with him, there was no answer at his apartment. All she felt was relief.

On Saturday, at ten o'clock in the morning, the security guard called Eve to tell her Matthew was in the lobby.

Her heart slammed against her chest. Oh, dear Lord. She looked a wreck. Matthew would take one look and know something was drastically wrong. Yet she could not escape seeing him. He was probably standing right there, listening to the guard talk to her. "Wait five minutes, then send him up," she said.

She raced into her bedroom. Within minutes, she had discarded her robe and nightgown and hurriedly dressed in shorts and T-shirt. She tore into her bathroom, splashed cold water on her face, whipped a brush through her hair and managed to get on her makeup—

paying particular attention to the dark circles—before the doorbell rang.

Please, God, you'd better help me pull this off, because you owe me one, she prayed as she walked out to the foyer and opened the door.

Even though she would have preferred postponing this meeting until she had better control of herself, the first peace she'd felt in days nearly overwhelmed her as Matthew, grinning, enveloped her in a bear hug.

After they'd hugged and kissed, he flung his arm around her shoulders and said, "Now, what's going on? Why haven't you gone to work in a week? And why haven't you called the doctor?"

"I'm going to kill Margaret," Eve said.

"C'mon, tell me."

If only she could. If only there were someone, anyone, she could unburden herself to. "Look, Matthew, it's nothing for you or anyone else to worry about. Really."

"You don't go to work for a week, and you think people aren't going to *worry?*" he said incredulously. "Aunt Eve, ordinarily you would go to work even if you had walking pneumonia! Now, what's the matter?"

"If you must know, I've just felt a little down, that's all."

"Down?" he said. "You?"

"Yes, me," Eve said, forcing a laugh. "I'm human. I get down just like anyone else."

By now they were sitting in the living room—Eve on the couch, Matthew sprawled in one of the big taupe leather armchairs. "But *why?* Last time I talked to you, you sounded really happy." He studied her closely. "Are you *sure* you're not sick?"

"I'm not sick."

"Then what is it? Did something happen at work?"

Eve could see he wasn't going to give up until she gave him some kind of answer. She decided to tell him as much of the truth as she could. "All right, Matthew, if it's going to stop you from worrying, I'll tell you. I've just been upset because, well, I met a man in Ohio that I—I liked a lot, and I had hopes that things might...might work out between us...but they didn't."

"Oh. Gee, I'm sorry." He studied her for a moment, then said thoughtfully, "You must have really liked him to be so broken up about this."

Eve swallowed. "Yes. I really liked him."

"Well, he must be crazy!"

Eve knew she could just keep quiet and let Matthew think whatever he wanted to think, but something in her wouldn't let his assumption go unchallenged. Even if he'd never know Mitch was his father, she didn't want Matthew thinking unkind thoughts about him. "It—it wasn't his fault," she said. "I'm the one who broke off the relationship."

Matthew frowned. "I don't understand."

When Matthew frowned like that, he looked so much like Mitch it tore at Eve's heart. Dear Lord, how was she going to live without him? "I can't explain. There were just some obstacles between us that I couldn't find a way to overcome." She forced herself to smile. "But I'm going to be okay. I'm through feeling sorry for myself. Onward and upward, right?"

"Right." But his eyes were reflective, and he didn't seem convinced.

"I love you for worrying, Matthew," she said softly. "But I'm a big girl. I've had disappointments before. And I'm sure I'll have others in the future."

After a moment, he grinned. "So I made the trip down here for nothing, is that what you're saying?"

"I'm glad you came." Now she smiled for real. "And since you're here, let's celebrate. Let's go out for brunch."

Later, sitting across from each other at Eve's favorite neighborhood deli, Matthew said, "Have you and Mom had a fight or something?"

For a moment, Eve couldn't breathe. "What makes you say that?"

He shrugged. "Last time I talked to her, I said something about you, and she made a funny comment. I figured maybe you'd said something to her about what we'd talked about—you know, trying to get her to get out and do something."

"Yes, well . . ." Her need to assure him overruled her dislike of misleading him. "She wasn't too happy with what I had to say."

He grimaced. "Sorry."

"It's not *your* fault."

"Yes, it is. I should have talked to her myself."

"Matthew, you did try to talk to her. You told me you did."

He sighed. "Maybe I should've tried harder."

Eve placed her hand over his. "Come on," she said softly. "You're not to blame for your mother's problems."

His mouth twisted. "You don't know everything."

She stiffened, immediately withdrawing her hand. "I've never pretended to know everything."

"No, no, Aunt Eve, that's not what I meant! I meant you don't know everything that happened between my mom and me."

Eve frowned. "I don't understand."

He looked down at his plate. "I feel guilty because I...I brought up that thing about...finding my birth parents again." His troubled gaze met hers. "I know I shouldn't have, especially with her being so unhappy right now, but...it's...it's important to me."

Oh, Matthew.

"I wish I could explain it to her. I know she thinks I won't love her anymore if I find my birth parents, but Aunt Eve, I don't really care about *seeing* them, or anything, I mean, if they're still alive. I just need to *know*. I think that'll satisfy me. Just knowing who they were and maybe why they gave me up."

There were so many things Eve wanted to say. But all she could do was nod.

"You and Mom and Gran will still be my family. You'll always be my family. I'll always love all of you. If I could just make her understand..." His voice trailed off. "But every time I talk about it, she goes ballistic. I guess I'd better just forget about it, huh?" He shrugged. "It's not such a big deal, is it?"

"I'm sorry, Matthew."

"Yeah, well, it's not your fault."

Yes, it is. This time, it really is.

For days after Eve left Maple Hills, Mitch walked around like a man possessed.

He was filled with an anger so great he thought he might explode.

He snapped at everyone, including Nicholas.

On Tuesday, Ted Jasper, a lawyer with whom Mitch was supposed to be negotiating a settlement, said, "I don't know what kind of bug you've got up your rear end, Sinclair, but whatever it is, get rid of it!"

On Wednesday, Jill said, "If you talk to me in that tone of voice one more time, *Mr. Sinclair*, I'm going to quit, and you can find yourself another dog to kick."

On Thursday, his father said, "Mitchell, maybe you should take another vacation. I think you need it."

On Friday, Nicholas said, "Dad, did I do something to make you mad?"

On Saturday, Mitch went to the gym and pummeled the punching bag for over an hour.

On Monday, everyone stared at Eve.

She knew they were staring, even though, when she looked in their direction, whoever the person was would hurriedly look away.

At ten o'clock, she presided over the staff meeting, which was unusually subdued, with none of the banter and good-natured ribbing she'd grown accustomed to. Finally she said, "Maybe I'd better fire the lot of you and hire some people with some enthusiasm to fill your jobs."

Everyone laughed a bit self-consciously, but Eve's remark broke the ice, and soon the staff was almost back to normal.

After the meeting, Chloe came into Eve's office and shut the door behind her. She plopped down into a chair and said, "All right. Spill it."

"Spill what?"

"Don't play dumb with me, Eve. I've known you too long. Something happened with the guy, right?"

"What guy?"

"C'mon, Eve..."

Eve stared at her assistant. Chloe's warm brown eyes were suffused with understanding. Suddenly, without warning, Eve's eyes filled with tears. Before she knew what was happening, Chloe had jumped up, come around the desk and put her arms around her.

Eve hadn't cried in front of anyone since she was a teenager. She was embarrassed that she was doing so now, but she couldn't seem to help herself. Everything—all the frustration and unhappiness and loneliness and misery came pouring out of her.

By the time she was through, she had almost blurted out the entire story. Her near-indiscretion horrified her.

"I'm sorry," she said. "I don't know what came over me."

Chloe smiled gently. "It's okay, Eve. I'm kind of glad to know you're human like the rest of us." Then she grimaced. "I'm sorry about your fella. Maybe you can work things out."

Eve shook her head. "No, Chloe, it's over. I've got to accept that and go on."

Nine days later, Mitch sat up long after Nicholas had gone to bed.

His anger had finally disappeared. Now he felt numb. Numb and miserable and lonelier than he had ever been.

What was he going to do with the rest of his life? he wondered. Nicholas would be gone in a couple of years, and then Mitch would be alone.

Alone.

Even the word sounded forlorn.

He closed his eyes and leaned his head back. *Eve, Eve, why did you leave me? Why couldn't you love me the way I love you?*

How could he have been so completely fooled? How could Eve have changed so much? He thought back, reliving every day and night they'd spent together. He replayed all the times they'd made love. All the conversations they'd had.

She hadn't been acting. He'd stake his life on that. She had been as happy with him as he'd been with her.

But if she hadn't been acting, then why had she said the things she'd said? There was something strange about the entire thing.

And if he hadn't been so hurt that night, he'd have realized it then.

Matthew called on Thursday, nearly two weeks since Eve had so hurriedly left Ohio. "Aunt Eve?" he said. "Would you mind if I brought Chris with me and we came down for the weekend?" Chris was Matthew's best friend.

"Of course I don't mind."

"Okay. We're gonna fly down and be there about noon tomorrow. Will you let the guard know?"

"Sure thing. Do you and Chris want to have dinner with me tomorrow night, or have you got plans?"

"We've got plans. Do you mind?"

"Of course not."

"But I'd love to spend Sunday with you. Chris'll be leaving early Sunday morning, but I could stay until Sunday night."

Eve smiled. "It's a date."

By the time the weekend arrived, Mitch concluded Eve had been lying to him. For some reason, she had been lying to him. Because she loved him. He knew she did. She simply could not have been faking her emotions.

Something had happened to cause her to lie, and he was going to get to the bottom of it.

Saturday afternoon he flew to New York.

On the way he thought about what his first move should be. He could not just walk up to her apartment and knock on the door. He knew that. First of all, she would not live in the kind of place you could walk up to. There would be some kind of doorman or guard, and each visitor would have to be announced. Mitch didn't want to take a chance on being announced. She might refuse to see him, and then what would he do? Flatten the guard and break down her door?

Think, he told himself.

Should he wait until Monday morning and go to her office? He immediately rejected the idea. First of all, he didn't want to talk to her with other people around. Secondly, she could refuse to see him there, too. Somehow Mitch couldn't see himself making a scene and pushing his way into her private office.

He spent the night alone in his hotel room, ordered a room service dinner and finally came up with a plan. Then, for the first time in days, he fell asleep minutes after his head hit the pillow.

The following morning, he awoke at six. He ordered coffee, then shaved and took a fast shower. He drank his coffee while he dressed.

By seven, he was downstairs.

At 7:15, he was in a cab, headed toward Eve's.

At 7:33, he was stationed across the street from her apartment building. Behind him was Central Park, already filling with early-morning joggers who were trying to beat the July heat.

He'd been right. There was a doorman standing under the canopied entrance to her building. There was also a security guard inside, because the guard opened the door about seven forty-five and said something to the doorman.

Mitch intended to watch the door until Eve came out. If she didn't come out today, she would be sure to come out tomorrow. Sooner or later, she would emerge, and when she did, he would not let her go until she agreed to talk to him.

For the next two and a half hours, at least a dozen people came out of her building: an older couple with a Welsh corgi on a leash, a younger couple who linked arms and walked off down the street, a young man with a duffel bag who hailed a cab. But no Eve.

Then, at a few minutes past ten, Mitch's wait was over.

His heart leaped when he saw her walk out the door. She looked so beautiful. She was wearing some kind of short, black casual dress that looked like a long tank top, black sandals, and her hair was tied back from her face with a black-and-white ribbon. She stopped to talk to the doorman, and Mitch didn't wait any longer.

He bounded across the street, ignoring the horns and catcalls of the cab drivers.

Eve hadn't seen him. She was turned, halfway facing the door.

Mitch reached the sidewalk, and the doorman looked at him curiously.

Just as Mitch opened his mouth to say her name, the front door opened again, and a young man emerged.

Mitch stared. For one heart-stopping moment, he thought he must be seeing things.

"May I help you, sir?" the doorman said.

Eve turned. Her startled gaze met Mitch's, and she gasped. Her face drained of color.

"Aunt Eve?" the young man said. "Are you all right?"

Mitch slowly looked at the young man again. No, he hadn't been seeing things. The young man standing there with the bewildered look on his face looked just like he'd looked the first time: a slightly older replica of Nicholas, right down to the incongruous streak of white hair.

Chapter Sixteen

"Mitch?" Eve whispered. Her brain refused to function. Her body refused to move.

Mitch's gaze was rooted to Matthew.

I can't believe this is happening, Eve thought. *This can't be happening.*

Mitch finally looked at her, and she could see all of the emotions, all of the questions, in his eyes.

Please, she begged him silently. *Please don't say anything here. Not in front of Matthew. Please.* Finally she managed to say, "You really surprised me, Mitch. I wasn't expecting you."

He nodded slowly. "I wanted to talk to you, so I...I took a chance." He glanced at Matthew, then met her gaze again. "I can see this isn't a good time."

Feeling as if this were a dream she would wake from at any moment, Eve said, "I was so shocked to see you, I've forgotten my manners." She reached back, touched

Matthew's arm. "Matthew, this is a friend of mine from Ohio, Mitch Sinclair. Mitch, this is my nephew, Matthew DelVecchio." She was proud of herself because her voice did not tremble, even though her insides were quaking.

Matthew smiled. He and Mitch shook hands, sizing each other up in the process. Eve's heart twisted as she watched them. A person would have to be blind not to see the resemblance. Even if Matthew hadn't looked so eerily like his half brother, how could Eve have imagined for even one moment that she could hide Matthew's paternity from Mitch?

Seeing them together—the same shaped head and hands, the same mouth, the same color of eyes—it was obvious they were father and son. And Eve knew, if they were to walk down the street together, their walks would be identical, too.

"It's nice to meet you, Mr. Sinclair," Matthew said. "So you're from Ohio, huh?"

Eve knew that Matthew had probably figured out Mitch was the man she'd been so torn up over.

"Yes. Your aunt and I are old friends."

Matthew nodded. His eyes were speculative.

"She tells me you're in pre-med," Mitch said. "At Harvard?"

"Yes."

"In your first year? Second year?"

"Second."

"That makes you what? Nineteen?"

"Yes, I was nineteen in March."

"Look," Eve said hurriedly—she *had* to stop this conversation, "we can't stand out here and talk. We...we were just going out for brunch, Mitch." *Oh, no, why did she say that? Now she'd have to invite*

Mitch to come, too. "Would . . . would you like to join us?"

"No, listen, Aunt Eve," Matthew said, "I know you two guys want to talk. Why don't I go over to the deli and get some breakfast myself? That way you and Mr. Sinclair can have some privacy for a while."

"Oh, Matthew, would you mind?" Eve said gratefully.

"Thanks, Matthew," Mitch said. "I *would* like to talk to your aunt alone."

Eve felt as if the planet were spinning out of control and the only thing she could do was hang on for dear life.

"See you guys later," Matthew said, waved his hand and walked off down the street.

Silently Eve and Mitch walked inside. She nodded at the security guard, who gave her a quizzical look but didn't say anything. They were silent in the elevator, too, but Eve knew the questions would come in a barrage the moment the apartment doors were closed behind them.

Sure enough, they were no sooner inside than Mitch said, "Matthew is my son, isn't he? Yours and mine."

Eve nodded. Tears clogged her throat.

He closed his eyes. "God, Eve," he whispered. "Why didn't you tell me?"

The tears spilled over, and she trembled violently. He hesitated a moment, then pulled her close, stroking her hair and murmuring, "It's okay. Calm down. Tell me now."

When her tears had slowed down enough so that she could talk, she said, "L-let's go sit down. I—I don't think I can stand up any longer."

She led the way into the living room. They sat on the couch and she told him everything.

How she had discovered she was pregnant.

How desperate she felt.

How she had called her brother, and what he and Mary Ann and her parents had eventually decided.

"But I don't understand. Why didn't you let me know?"

"How could I?" she cried. "You were already married to Carolyn when I found out. What could you have done? If we could've been married, that would have been one thing. But we couldn't have, and, God, Mitch, I was only seventeen! I couldn't face that kind of scandal. Think of it. You were the mayor's son! Besides, I was afraid of what my father and brother would do if they knew who you were. They would have come after you and caused a lot of trouble."

"You mean they didn't know?" Mitch said incredulously. "What did you tell them?"

Eve grimaced. "I told them the father was a married man, and they thought..." She swallowed. "They assumed I'd taken up with someone married."

He thought for a while, then finally sighed and said, "All right. I understand why you couldn't say anything then, but why didn't you tell me when you came back to Ohio in June?"

"I wanted to, but long ago, I made a promise to Tony and Mary Ann that I would never tell Matthew I was his mother. Then, after I saw you again...and fell in love again...I knew I couldn't marry you without telling you, so when I came back to New York that first time—before Nicholas came home—I approached Mary Ann about it. Well, she went a little nuts. She...she screamed at me, and she refused to release me from my promise.

Quite honestly, Mitch, I was afraid of what she'd do if I opposed her." Eve ducked her head. "I—I hate to admit this, but I actually considered marrying you and not telling you, but then I met Nicholas. And I knew there was no way. The minute you met Matthew you would know. So would everyone else."

He stared at her. Pain clouded his eyes. "So you weren't ever going to tell me."

"I'm sorry," she said inadequately.

He stood abruptly. "But I had a *right* to know!"

"A right to know!" Suddenly all Eve's own feelings of guilt disappeared, and a healthy dose of anger replaced it. She stood, too. "You forfeited all your rights when you dumped me, Mitch!"

"You've never forgiven me, have you? Even when you said you had, down deep, you were angry. You still are."

They glared at each other, the few feet between them suddenly seeming like an unbreachable chasm.

But a moment later, his shoulders slumped. "Oh, hell, who can blame you?" he said wearily. "You're right. I *did* forfeit all my rights."

Her anger evaporated as quickly as it had formed. Assigning blame wouldn't change anything. Making him feel bad wouldn't change anything. Besides, she *had* forgiven him. They were both at fault here. He hadn't forced her to have sex with him. She had been just as irresponsible as he'd been. "Mitch, you'll never know how much I wanted to tell you, but I couldn't break my promise." With her eyes, she begged for his understanding. "I'm sorry, Mitch. I just didn't know what else to do."

"So that's why you left Ohio. Because you'd seen Nicholas and knew you wouldn't be able to keep your secret."

"Yes."

"Well, now I know. So where do we go from here?"

Eve swallowed. "I—I don't know. I still feel shell-shocked."

His eyes softened. "Come here," he said, reaching for her. She trembled as he drew her into his arms. When his lips met hers, all the barriers they'd raised that afternoon tumbled from the force of their feelings.

They kissed with the greed and hunger of starving people who have finally been fed, with the desperation of drowning people who have been thrown a rope, with the passion of zealots who have found a receptive audience.

They clung together, kissing as if a rationing system were going to go into effect, and these kisses had to last them the rest of their lives.

When they were finally sated, Mitch said, "Do you love me, Eve?"

"With all my heart."

"And do you want to marry me?"

"More than anything in the world."

He sighed. "Okay. At least we've settled that much. Now let's sit down and decide how we're going to handle the rest of it."

Eve let him lead her back to the couch, but her mind churned. He sounded as if he thought they could still get married. As if there were no more obstacles.

He frowned. "Now what's wrong?"

"Well, I just don't see how we can get married. I mean, there's still the problem of Matthew...and

Nicholas. There's no way we could keep them from meeting each other.''

He stared at her. "Of course they're going to meet each other. For God's sake, Eve, they're *brothers*. We don't have the right to keep them apart.'' Slowly awareness dawned, and once again anger fired his eyes. "Did you actually think you could *still* keep this whole mess a secret? That I would go along with not telling Matthew I'm his father?''

Eve bit her bottom lip.

"That's exactly what you thought! Well, no way is that going to happen. Matthew may not want to have anything to do with me when he finds out I'm his father, but I'm willing to take that chance.''

"But Mary Ann—''

"I don't care what your sister-in-law says. There aren't going to be any more secrets. It's time for the truth. In fact, there's no time like the present. I think we should tell him when he gets back here.''

"No, Mitch, no! Please. I implore you! We can't say anything to Matthew today. I've got to talk to Mary Ann first!''

He looked at her. Finally he nodded. "All right. You can talk to Mary Ann. We'll both talk to her. Together. But,'' he added, a warning glint in his eyes, "no matter what she says, I'm not going to change my mind.''

"He's the guy, isn't he? The one you told me about?''

Eve whirled. "Oh, Matthew, you startled me!''

Mitch had gone into the bathroom, and Eve had come out to the kitchen to put on a pot of coffee. She hadn't heard Matthew come in.

"Sorry,'' he said sheepishly.

"Yes, he's the man.''

"I like him."

Eve smiled. "You don't even know him." But her heart refused to listen to her cautionary words, because it lifted at his approval.

"Are things gonna work out for you two?" Matthew said. He dumped a bag on the counter. "I brought back some bagels."

"Oh, thanks. Well, I'm not sure if they're going to or not. We're . . . we're working on it."

"Looks to me like he really cares about you. He came all the way here just to talk to you, and all."

Eve nodded. "Yes, he cares, but there are still some problems. We'll see," she said vaguely.

"Look, I was thinking. Why don't I catch an earlier flight back? That way you two can be alone."

"No, Matthew, I don't want you to leave early."

"I don't, either," said Mitch, walking into the kitchen. "I'd enjoy getting to know the nephew Eve has spoken so highly of."

Matthew grinned. "Well, if you're sure . . ."

"We're sure," Mitch and Eve said together.

Mitch decided that Sunday was one of the best days of his life. For the next four hours, he basked in the knowledge that the handsome, intelligent, mannerly young man sitting there in Eve's apartment was his son—the product of the passion and love they'd shared so many years ago.

And Eve. Even though she was misguided in her loyalty to her sister-in-law, Mitch loved her so much. She'd gone through a lot on his account, and he knew he had much to make up to her. But he would.

All the obstacles between them, save one, were gone.

And that obstacle would be removed tomorrow when they went to Connecticut to see Mary Ann.

Matthew left at four. Eve hugged him tightly. "Take care," she said. "I'll talk to you soon."

The men shook hands.

"It was nice meeting you, sir," Matthew said. "I know my aunt's glad you came." He smiled. "I hope we'll see each other again sometime."

Mitch swallowed over the sudden lump in his throat. For a moment, he was too choked up to speak. "Oh, we'll see each other again, son," he said. "I'm sure of that."

After Matthew was gone, Mitch put his arms around her. "He's a wonderful kid, Eve."

She touched his cheek. "He takes after his father."

"How much farther is it?" Mitch said.

"Just over the next rise," Eve said. It was just before noon on Monday, and they had driven up to Connecticut in Eve's Mercedes.

The evening before, Mitch had gone back to his hotel, packed and checked out, then taken a cab back to Eve's, where he'd spent the night.

Lying in bed in Mitch's arms, making love when she'd thought she would never make love with him again, had been a bittersweet pleasure, because she hadn't been able to turn her mind off. In the back of her brain—constant and niggling like a nagging toothache—was the worry about what Mary Ann would say or do when they saw her.

In just minutes, Eve would know.

"That's it, that's the house," Eve said, pointing to a large two-story Colonial that sat far back on a substantial, heavily wooded lot. The house had been Eve's first major purchase after the initial success of Eden.

They pulled into the driveway.

"What if she's not home?" Eve said.

"Then we'll wait," Mitch said. He turned off the ignition and reached for her hand, giving it an encouraging squeeze. "Don't worry. It's going to be all right."

"You don't know Mary Ann," Eve murmured.

"I don't understand why you're so worried. After all, what can she do?"

"She can turn Matthew against me. And you. That's what she can do."

Mitch's expression told Eve he hadn't thought about that contingency. He nodded soberly. "Well, then we'll just have to tread cautiously."

They walked up to the front door and rang the bell.

Mary Ann answered on the second ring. Her startled eyes betrayed her shock at seeing Eve, and the blood that drained from her face told Eve she immediately guessed who Mitch was.

Eve realized her sister-in-law had probably always secretly feared this day. "Hello, Mary Ann," she said, compassion softening her voice. "May we come in?"

Mary Ann, eyes wide and fearful, held the door open. Her gaze met Eve's briefly before she ushered them into the living room.

"Mary Ann, this is Mitch Sinclair. Mitch, this is my sister-in-law, Mary Ann DelVecchio."

Mitch and Mary Ann exchanged innocuous pleasantries, and Eve could see how Mary Ann studied him. Yes, Mary Ann definitely suspected Mitch's identity.

They all sat down.

"I know why you're here," Mary Ann said. Her voice trembled. She looked at Mitch. "Y-you're Matthew's father, aren't you?"

"Yes, I am."

Her mouth twisted as her gaze turned to Eve. "How could you? You promised!"

"Mary Ann, I didn't break my promise. Mitch came to New York and Matthew was there. When he saw him, he immediately knew."

Mary Ann's face crumpled, and she buried her face in her hands.

"Oh, God," Eve whispered. She got up, went over to the couch where Mary Ann sat and put her arms around her. "I'm sorry, Mary Ann. But it's going to be okay. Really it is."

Mary Ann's body shuddered violently. Eve's gaze met Mitch's over Mary Ann's head. *See? I told you. This isn't going to be easy.* Eve felt close to tears herself. She continued to hold her sister-in-law and murmur comforting words.

Finally Mary Ann drew a shaky breath and sat up. She wiped her eyes and blew her nose. "I'm sorry," she whispered, not meeting Eve's eyes.

"Don't be silly." Eve took Mary Ann's hand. She held it firmly. "I know this was a shock. I also know how you must feel."

Mary Ann looked up. Her dark eyes were filled with pain. "You don't know how I feel. You couldn't. I—I've been so ashamed of myself. I—I wanted to call you, but I just couldn't. I'm sorry I said such awful things to you that day. Y-you were right. I didn't mean half of them. I—I was just so angry! I've been angry ever since Tony died." Her eyes filled with tears again. "Why did he leave me, Eve? Why?"

"Oh, Mary Ann..."

Mitch got up. "Maybe I should leave for a while."

"No, no," Mary Ann said. "You don't have to leave." She blew her nose again. "I'm okay." She reached for Eve's hand again. "That day? I was scared, too. I mean, you're so smart and so pretty and everyone likes you." She swallowed. "Matthew thinks you're perfect, and I—I guess I thought if he knew you were his *real* mother, he wouldn't love me anymore."

"Oh, Mary Ann, you'll *always* be his real mother. It's just like you said. You're the one who sat up with him at night, not me. You're the one who was here every day after school, not me. He knows that."

"Do you really think so?"

"I know so." Eve decided it was time for the whole truth. "And to be completely honest with you, I'm scared, too."

"You?" Mary Ann said.

Eve nodded. "Maybe Matthew will be angry with me. Did you ever think of that?"

Mary Ann stared at her.

"Maybe he won't want to have anything to do with me, or Mitch."

"I—I never realized..." Mary Ann said. "But of course, you're right. You're taking a chance on losing him, too, aren't you?"

"Yes."

Mary Ann sighed. "But he has a right to know, doesn't he?"

Eve nodded. "Yes, he does."

Mary Ann studied Mitch. "Matthew looks like you," she said softly.

"He's a wonderful kid," Mitch said. "You and your husband did a great job raising him."

Mary Ann smiled. "Now I see where Matthew got his charm."

"We thought we'd fly up to Boston tomorrow," Eve said. "Do you want to come with us?"

Mary Ann hesitated. "No, this is between you two and Matthew."

They talked for a while, then Mary Ann insisted they have lunch with her, so they trooped out to the kitchen, and Mitch wandered out to the backyard and looked around while Eve helped Mary Ann fix tuna salad for sandwiches.

After lunch, Mary Ann showed Mitch around the house. He stood in Matthew's room for a long time, fingering the worn books in the maple bookcase and the scarred desk and the few toys left over from childhood. He walked around and studied the pictures on the walls.

"Would you like one of his graduation pictures?" Mary Ann asked.

Mitch's face lit up. "Would you mind?"

She shook her head.

About three o'clock, they said their goodbyes. Eve and Mary Ann hugged tightly.

"Thank you," Eve said. "You don't know how much today means to me."

"I love you," Mary Ann whispered. "Do you forgive me?"

"I love you, too," Eve said. Her eyes felt misty again. Honestly! For someone who rarely cried, she'd shed enough tears lately to fill a small lake. "And there's nothing to forgive."

"Now are you *sure* you don't mind waiting in the car while I go in?" Eve said.

Mitch shook his head. "No. It's right that you talk to him alone first."

So Eve, her stomach a mass of butterflies, left Mitch in their rental car and walked up to Matthew's apartment building in Cambridge by herself.

Matthew lived in a four-plex. His apartment was on the second floor. Eve walked up to the door and pressed his buzzer. She had called him from the airport to let him know she was coming, but she hadn't told him why, just that she had something important to discuss with him. He had sounded happy, and she knew he probably thought she'd come to tell him she was getting married, or something like that.

What was he going to say? *Oh, please, God, let him be happy about this.*

Matthew buzzed her in, and she climbed the stairs to the second floor. Before she'd even reached the top, he'd flung open his door and stood there grinning at her.

"Hi," she said.

"Hi. Boy, you sure look great!" His approving gaze took in her violet sleeveless dress and matching sandals.

"Thanks."

"I'll bet I can guess what you've come to tell me," he said happily as she walked into the apartment.

She smiled as she looked around. The apartment was a mess. Not dirty, just messy.

Matthew grabbed up a stack of books and papers from an easy chair and said, "Here. Sit here. Sorry about the mess." He reached for one of the dinette chairs and straddled it. He grinned expectantly.

Eve took a deep breath. Now that the moment was upon her, she felt terrified. What if Matthew was angry over her revelation? What if he resented her? What if he felt betrayed by all the years she'd kept this from him?

Too late now.

The grin slid off his face. He frowned. "What? Is something wrong?"

"No." *Tell him!* "No," she said more firmly. "At least I don't think so. And I hope you won't."

He waited, his hazel eyes puzzled.

"Matthew, I know who your birth mother is."

His eyes widened. "You do?"

Eve nodded. "I—I've always known."

"You . . . you've *always* known?"

Eve wet her lips. "Yes."

He frowned. "But . . . does that mean Mom has always known, too?"

"Yes. And your dad."

He stared at her. "I don't understand . . ."

She looked deep into those eyes she loved so much. Her heart was thumping hard, and those damned tears that never seemed very far from the surface these days threatened again. "I'm your birth mother, Matthew."

For a long moment, the room was silent. Then, slowly, he said, "*You're* my birth mother?"

Incapable of speech, she only nodded.

He shook his head in disbelief. "I—I can't believe it. Why didn't you tell me? All these years . . . why didn't you tell me?"

"I—I wanted to, believe me, I wanted to. But your mom and dad and I, we'd made an agreement. They felt, we all felt, it would be in your best interests not to be pulled two ways. W-we wanted you to have a secure childhood. I—I promised them I would never tell you."

"Then why are you telling me *now!*" Without warning, his face twisted. "All these years, I felt so guilty because I always loved you best. More than my mom. More than my dad. And you...you didn't want me." His eyes were filled with pain.

"That's not true!" she cried.

"Sure it is. You gave me away. Here, all this time, I was feeling sorry for my...my birth mother, thinking she was some poor girl who didn't have any choice...but you...you could have kept me."

Eve bit her bottom lip as her tears spilled over.

"Why?" he said. "Just tell me why you did it."

"Matthew, please try to understand. I was only seventeen. I wasn't married, and y-your father wasn't free to marry me. I didn't know what else to do." Her voice broke. "I've always loved you more than anyone else in the world. What I did, I did because I thought it was best for you." *Please, please understand.*

He stared at her. "How could it be best for me not to know the truth?"

Eve didn't know what to say. She realized that anything she said would only make it seem as if she had been trying to protect herself. I know you're angry...and I don't blame you...but I hope, after you've had time to think about it, you'll be able to forgive me." She swiped at her tears, mad at herself for breaking down. She didn't want him to feel sorry for her.

He swallowed. "I—I'm sorry. I wish I didn't feel this way. I just can't seem to help it."

Eve got up and walked over to him. "I love you, Matthew. You've always meant more to me than anyone. Please don't shut me out now. Please try to understand." He looked at her for a long moment, and gradually, the anger faded from his eyes.

"I love you, too," he said, and she could see he was trying not to break down, too.

She reached up to hug him, and his arms closed around her, pulling her close.

"Please say you forgive me." His voice was muffled as he said, "I—I always knew there was something special between us."

It was going to be okay. *Thank you, God. Thank you.*

Eventually Matthew released her, and they both sat down again.

"I want to hear everything," he said. "From the beginning. Don't leave out anything."

Eve gave him an abbreviated version of the events leading up to his conception and how the decision for him to be adopted by Tony and Mary Ann had come about.

"So who is this guy who fathered me? Do you know what happened to him?" Matthew said.

"Well," Eve said. "That's the other thing I wanted to tell you. Yes, I do know what happened to him. In fact, he's outside right now, waiting to see you."

Matthew jumped up so fast he knocked over the chair. "He's outside! Why didn't you tell me?"

Eve stood. "I wasn't sure how you'd take the news." She met his gaze. "You know him, Matthew."

"What?"

"Can't you guess? It's Mitch. Mitch is your father."

Years later, when Eve relived this moment, she knew the look on Matthew's face would be what she would remember with the most clarity. It was a priceless mixture of shock and confusion and a slowly dawning elation.

Hand in hand, she and Matthew walked outside.

The hot July sun beat down. A pretty blonde whizzed by on a ten-speed bike. From down the street came the sound of someone playing the piano.

And in the midst of all these ordinary and mundane sounds and activities, Mitchell Emerson Sinclair and Matthew John DelVecchio, father and son, embraced for the first time.

Eve watched them, her heart full to bursting.

As they slowly drew apart, Mitch's gaze met hers, and he smiled, beckoning to her with his hand.

She walked slowly forward, into the circle of their warm and loving arms, these two men she loved most in the entire world. She knew there would be other problems to overcome, other hurdles to cross, but together, the three of them could weather anything.

Epilogue

Eve looked around contentedly. Everything was ready. The tree twinkled with hundreds of tiny white lights. Earlier, Mitch had built a fire in the fireplace, and now the flames leaped and danced merrily.

In the kitchen, the turkey was roasting in the oven. Christmas carols were playing softly on the CD player. All the presents were wrapped and waiting. Even the weather had cooperated, and snow fell gently outside.

And best of all, in just minutes, Matthew and Mary Ann would be there to celebrate this first Christmas Eve together in Ohio as a united family.

She heard footsteps, and Mitch entered the living room. He looked so handsome, she thought. Of course, she was prejudiced. She thought her husband was the most attractive man she'd ever met.

He slipped his hand around her waist and bent down to nuzzle her neck.

"Mmm," he said. "You smell good."

She smiled, raising her face for his kiss. "You taste good," she said after the leisurely kiss was over.

Just then, the doorbell rang, and simultaneously, Nicholas's footsteps could be heard bounding down the stairs.

Mitch went to the door. First Mary Ann, then Matthew, snow dotting their dark hair and shoulders, cheeks red from the cold, eyes sparkling and smiles bright, entered. Each was loaded down with packages.

Seconds later, Nicholas had joined them, and the five of them greeted and hugged and laughed in happy anticipation. Eve watched with a lump in her throat as the brothers slapped each other on the back. She felt this way each time she saw them together, and wondered if she'd ever get over the miracle of it. From the first moment they'd met, Nicholas and Matthew had loved each other. In fact, the bond between them was incredible— something she could never have imagined. No one, seeing them together, would ever dream they had only known each other months.

Soon the newcomers had shed their coats, and they settled down to enjoy each other's company. They drank eggnog and talked, then moved into the dining room where they stuffed themselves with turkey and all the trimmings. After dinner, the boys offered to clean up, saying, "You guys go sit down. We can handle it."

"No, no, no," Mary Ann protested. "I'm helping, too."

"What, you don't trust us?" Matthew teased. But he gave in good-naturedly and allowed her to come with them.

From the living room, where Eve sat close to Mitch, her head on his shoulder, she listened to the banter and laughter coming from the kitchen.

She sighed. Her life was so perfect, it almost scared her. Anything this good shouldn't last, but each day, it only seemed to get better. And now, it was going to get better still.

"Mitch," she whispered. "I have something for you that I want to give you before the others come back."

He kissed her forehead. "All right. Where is it?"

She turned her head so she could see into his eyes. Taking his hand, she placed it over her stomach. "Here. It's in here."

For a moment, he didn't react. Then, eyes widening in delight, he let out a whoop. "Eve! Are you sure? You're pregnant?"

She smiled. "Yes. I'm sure. I even went to the doctor the other day, and they did an ultrasound. I'm seven weeks, and everything looks good."

He crushed her to him. "I never thought I could be this happy," he said against her temple. "You've given me so much, and now you're going to give me more."

Eve wanted to cry. She felt the same way, only it was Mitch who had given *her* so much.

A little later, they were joined by the boys and Mary Ann, and Eve shyly told them her news. She wasn't sure how they would take the disclosure, but she needn't have worried. All three seemed thrilled.

"Boy, this baby's gonna be really spoiled," Nicholas said.

"I hope it's a little girl," Matthew said, a teasing twinkle in his eyes, "because one bratty little brother is enough."

Everybody laughed, even Nicholas.

"And Mary Ann," Eve said, "Mitch and I would be honored to have you be our baby's godmother. In fact, I was hoping you could come and stay for a while after the baby's born and give me a hand."

Later that night, lying in Mitch's arms, Eve thought about life. Her life, and how it had come full circle. The new life inside her and what it would mean to all of them.

She sighed in contentment.

Mitch's arms tightened around her. "You asleep?" he whispered.

"No."

"What're you thinking about?"

She told him.

He kissed her ear. His hand moved down to cover her stomach. "Have I ever told you how much I love you?" he murmured.

Eve smiled, turning in his arms so she could see his eyes. "Yes, but tell me again."

And so he did.

* * * * *

Silhouette®

SPECIAL EDITION™®

COMING NEXT MONTH

Celebration 1000! Begins With:
#991 MAGGIE'S DAD—Diana Palmer
Celebration 1000!
Returning home, Antonia Hayes was determined not to fall
again for Powell Long. But the single dad was sexier than
ever—and he had *definite* ideas about their reunion!

#992 MORGAN'S SON—Lindsay McKenna
Morgan's Mercenaries: Love and Danger
Rescuing a little boy hit close to home for high-risk expert
Sabra Jacobs. Mercenary Craig Talbot knew they faced perilous
odds on this mission—but the real danger was losing his heart
to her....

#993 CHILD OF MINE—Jennifer Mikels
Ambitious and practical Alex Kane needed one thing: to get
his son back. But that meant marrying carefree and outgoing
Carly Mitchell, and once they'd said their vows, it was obvious
this marriage would *not* be in name only!

#994 THE DADDY QUEST—Celeste Hamilton
Precocious Zane McPherson was on a quest to find a daddy
who'd be the perfect match for his mom, Holly. Tough cop
Brooks Casey never entertained the idea of being a family
man—but one look at Holly had Brooks changing his mind!

#995 LOGAN'S BRIDE—Christine Flynn
The Whitaker Brides/Holiday Elopement
Samantha Gray knew Logan Whitaker was trouble the moment
she saw him. She'd only wanted a secure future for her children,
but falling for the sexy rancher seemed inevitable—and resisting
his tempting offer of marriage was even harder....

#996 BRAVE HEART—Brittany Young
No-nonsense lawyer Rory Milbourne didn't believe in fate. But
Daniel Blackhawk knew it was destiny that had brought Rory
to him—and that she was the other half of his heart he'd been
waiting all his life to find....

Take 4 bestselling love stories FREE

Plus get a FREE surprise gift!

Special Limited-time Offer

Mail to Silhouette Reader Service™

3010 Walden Avenue
P.O. Box 1867
Buffalo, N.Y. 14269-1867

YES! Please send me 4 free Silhouette Special Edition® novels and my free surprise gift. Then send me 6 brand-new novels every month, which I will receive months before they appear in bookstores. Bill me at the low price of $3.12 each plus 25¢ delivery and applicable sales tax, if any.* That's the complete price and a savings of over 10% off the cover prices—quite a bargain! I understand that accepting the books and gift places me under no obligation ever to buy any books. I can always return a shipment and cancel at any time. Even if I never buy another book from Silhouette, the 4 free books and the surprise gift are mine to keep forever.

235 BPA A96Y

Name	(PLEASE PRINT)	
Address	Apt. No.	
City	State	Zip

This offer is limited to one order per household and not valid to present Silhouette Special Edition™ subscribers. *Terms and prices are subject to change without notice. Sales tax applicable in N.Y.

USPED-995   ©1990 Harlequin Enterprises Limited

Become a Privileged Woman,

You'll be entitled to all these *Free Benefits.* And *Free Gifts,* too.

To thank you for buying our books, we've designed an exclusive FREE program called *PAGES & PRIVILEGES™.* You can enroll with just one Proof of Purchase, and get the kind of luxuries that, until now, you could only read about.

BIG HOTEL DISCOUNTS

A privileged woman stays in the finest hotels. And so can you—at up to 60% off! Imagine standing in a hotel check-in line and watching as the guest in front of you pays $150 for the same room that's only costing you $60. Your *Pages & Privileges* discounts are good at Sheraton, Marriott, Best Western, Hyatt and thousands of other fine hotels all over the U.S., Canada and Europe.

FREE DISCOUNT TRAVEL SERVICE

A privileged woman is always jetting to romantic places.

When _you_ fly, just make one phone call for the lowest published airfare at time of booking— <u>or double the difference back!</u>

PLUS—you'll get a $25 voucher to use the first time you book a flight AND <u>5% cash back on every ticket you buy thereafter through the travel service!</u>